"Get A Grip, Princess. You've Seen Me In My Skivvies Before,"

Mac said lazily.

"Not an experience I wanted to repeat," Marisa snapped. Face flaming, she added, "I suppose your behaving with the least bit of common decency is too much to expect."

"Hey, I was wet. You want me to sleep in damp clothes and catch my death?"

"It's a thought."

"You know, the most sensible thing would be for us to cuddle together to conserve body heat."

"In your dreams, Mahoney."

Yeah, in my dreams, Mac thought. *If only she knew.*

Dear Reader:

News flash!

The Branigans Are Back!

All of you who have written over the years to say how much you love Leslie Davis Guccione's BRANIGAN BROTHERS will be thrilled and pleased that this rambunctious family is back with *Branigan's Break*.

More Fun from Lass Small!

We start the New Year with a fun-filled *Man of the Month* from one of your favorite writers. Don't miss *A Nuisance*, which is what our man makes of himself this month!

The Return of Diana Mars!

So many readers have wondered, "Where is Diana Mars?" This popular author took a break from writing, but we're excited that she's now writing for Silhouette Desire with *Peril in Paradise*.

Christmas in January!

For those of you who can't get enough of the holidays, please don't let Suzannah Davis's charming *A Christmas Cowboy* get away.

Mystery and Danger...

In Modean Moon's *Interrupted Honeymoon*.

Baby, Baby...

In Shawna Delacorte's *Miracle Baby*.

So start the New Year right with Silhouette Desire!

With all best wishes for a great 1995,

Lucia Macro
Senior Editor

Please address questions and book requests to:
Silhouette Reader Service
U.S.: 3010 Walden Ave., P.O. Box 1325, Buffalo, NY 14269
Canadian: P.O. Box 609, Fort Erie, Ont. L2A 5X3

SUZANNAH DAVIS
A CHRISTMAS COWBOY

SILHOUETTE *Desire*®
™
Published by Silhouette Books
America's Publisher of Contemporary Romance

 SILHOUETTE BOOKS

ISBN 0-373-05903-5

A CHRISTMAS COWBOY

SUZANNAH DAVIS

Award-winning author Suzannah Davis is a Louisiana native who loves small-town life, daffodils and writing stories full of love and laughter. Firm believers in happy endings, she and her husband have three children. *A Christmas Cowboy* is her fifteenth novel.

For Brian, Jill and Brad

Special Thanks to
A Martinez
and the cast and crew of "Santa Barbara"

One

Could a mother be charged with kidnapping her own son?

With a cry of frustration and fear, Marisa Rourke gave up her futile attempts to start a fire in the rustic hunting lodge's massive stone fireplace. A kerosene lantern illuminated the small figure asleep in a pile of blankets on the old leather sofa. Bending over him, Marisa stroked her five-year-old son's straight sandy hair. The golden tint was identical to her own, a happy coincidence of Nicky's adoption.

To her relief, his cheeks were warm and his breathing deep and easy. Love flooded Marisa, a feeling so powerful she had to close her eyes. It was followed immediately by a surge of fierce protectiveness. Nicky was hers. *Hers*. And no one was going to take him away from her!

But how long before hypothermia became a threat to a small child? Outside, the December blizzard of the century had blown down all the power lines crossing the California High Sierras, and now the emergency generator refused to crank, giving the spacious, two-story log dwelling with its wide banks of wraparound porches all the characteristics of an icebox. Since cowboys were Nicky's latest obsession, bedding down in front of the fireplace like ranch hands sleeping around a campfire had suited him just fine. In fact, so far, Nicky Latimore had found everything about this unexpected adventure with his mother perfectly charming.

Marisa wished her own feelings were as uncomplicated. A week ago, her life had been ... well, if not exactly perfect, at least contented. Despite her industrialist husband's death in a car accident three years ago, she was managing, juggling her booming acting career as Dinah Dillman on "Time Won't Tell," TV's most popular daytime drama, and her duties as spokesperson for the Adopt-a-Child Foundation with the demands and joys of single parenthood. Until reporter Marcus Craig "Mac" Mahoney had bulled his way back into her life.

Even after ten years, she hadn't been ready. Tall, sable-haired, everything about the tough investigative journalist from his changeable hazel green eyes to his ex-boxer's physique had been so familiar Marisa could have wept. Instead, Mac's scandalous accusations during the "Jackie Horton Live" television talk show regarding the illegal adoption racket of Dr. Franco Morris had turned her into a desperate runaway.

Again.

Shaking off a chill that bit deeper than the outside temperature, Marisa tucked Nicky's blankets closer, reliving her panic upon learning that Elsie Powers, a Louisiana native now living in nearby Riverside, was claiming the good doctor had stolen her infant son—stolen Nicky!—under false pretenses and emotional duress. And Elsie wanted him back.

That's why Marisa had run, escaping from Los Angeles with her child in her housekeeper's anonymous sedan, eaving behind the paparazzi, her agent, her lawyers and the police. Like a wounded animal, she'd come to ground in the same secluded mountain hideaway that had been her sanctuary the last time Mac Mahoney had shattered her world. Only this time, there was even more at stake.

With a shudder of apprehension, Marisa swung a quilt around her shoulders and went back to work on the obstinate fire. Outside, the wind howled.

It was the wind, wasn't it? Straightening, Marisa listened hard. Something was different, she realized. Had the tenor of that inhuman wailing changed somehow? She thought uneasily about wolves, then wrenched her galloping imagination back under control. She and Nicky were safe inside the lodge—except perhaps from frostbite if she didn't get the fire going! There was no reason to fear—

A thump sounded on the porch, and Marisa surged to her feet. A three-sided balcony opening onto the second-floor bedrooms overlooked the large den, the base of its staircase spilling into the foyer at the front of the lodge. From her vantage in front of the fireplace, Marisa could see directly into the shadowy hall. Something struck the front door, making it vibrate on its hinges. Her heart leapt to her throat. With a quick glance at Nicky's sleeping form, she gathered her courage, picked up the heavy cast-iron poker from the hearth and went to investigate.

The moment she reached the door, it rattled violently again, and she jumped back in alarm. What kind of animal would attack a human stronghold? And then she heard it: faint, wind-whipped echoes above the banshee scream of air. No wolf ever sounded like that—except the two-legged kind!

Warily, Marisa peeked through the heavy curtain covering the window beside the front door. The movement drew the attention of the snow-covered figure on the porch. A ferocious face glazed with ice and snow glared at her from the depths of a parka's fur-lined hood. "Dammit, Marisa, open up!" he roared. "I'm freezing!"

The blood drained from her face.

Mac.

He was mad as hell and getting angrier by the minute.

Raising his gloved fist, Mac Mahoney pounded on the lodge door again. Half-blinded by driving sleet, lungs seared by the frigid wind, feet numb inside his boots after a mile-long trek from where his Jeep sat bogged in a snowbank, he was in no mood for any of Marisa Rourke's foolishness. By God, the woman had already caused him enough trouble to last a lifetime!

The door creaked open a bare two inches. "Go away!"

He caught it just before it clicked shut in his face. Now he was furious. Shoving his shoulder against the door like a linebacker, he felt the momentary resistance of her weight on the other side, then he barreled through, flinging it wide open. A mountaineer reaching the summit of Mount Everest couldn't have been more triumphant. Until he saw the poker.

"Hey!" He ducked the blow she aimed at his head.

"Get out!"

"Are you *nuts?*"

"Not crazy enough to tolerate the likes of *you.*" Bundled in turtleneck and Scandinavian sweater, Marisa threw back her shoulder-length hair and glared at him, her eyes like blue ice. Snow laced with sleet blew in through the open doorway. "Get the hell out."

Exasperated, Mac shoved back the hood of his green, multipocketed parka, wiping ice crystals from his dark eyebrows. "It's snowing like the devil out there!"

"I don't care if you fall off a glacier." The knuckles of her hand grasping the poker turned white. "I'm warning you...."

Mac couldn't help it. He laughed. Until the swipe she took at him caught him sharply on the top of the shoulder. Enraged, Mac sprang, catching her wrist and pinning her against the wall.

"Drop it!" The padding of his thick parka had saved him from major damage, but he spoke through teeth gritted with pain. Stubbornly she held on to the poker, her angry breaths pushing her breasts against his chest. The air was charged with the smell of snow and fury.

"You aren't welcome here, Mahoney. Get it?"

"I didn't spend the past hour slogging uphill on foot in this mess to freeze to death. Let go." He squeezed harder.

She gave a cry, and her hand opened. The heavy poker clanged to the floor. Without releasing her, Mac kicked the front door shut. After the scream of the wind, the near silence was deafening. Her eyes glittered. "You are such a bastard."

"So I'm told." Showing his teeth, he leaned in closer. Even through his sodden, bulky clothing, he could feel her heat, smell the intoxicating scent of her perfume. His belly clenched in response, and the unwelcome sensation made him furious all over again. "So be warned. You try anything like that again, I won't be so forgiving."

Her lip curled, showing clearly what she thought of the quality of his mercy. "What are you doing here?"

"Better question, what are you?"

"I—" Her lashes lowered. "Vacationing."

"Huh. More like running away. Again." His mouth twisted in contempt. He released her and stepped back to strip out of his wet coat. "That's always been your answer to everything, hasn't it, Marisa?"

Her expression wavered.

Guilty, Mac thought. *She's guilty as hell.*

He cast a glance at the shadowy interior of the lodge—heavy wood-and-stone construction, oversize furnishings, the requisite Indian blankets and antler trophies strategically positioned on the log walls. The masculine environment was at odds with Marisa's slender femininity.

"So this is where you disappeared to ten years ago. Quite an interesting choice of refuge for a poor little rich girl, isn't it?"

Her chin came up. "Save your insults, Mahoney. You don't know anything about me—you never did! How did you find me?"

"Just played a hunch. It didn't take a rocket scientist to figure out you'd seek sanctuary at your *Uncle* Paul's."

"You didn't figure it out before."

His look was steady. "I didn't try." God, the satisfaction of saying that! After all these years with the acid eating away at his gut, to be able to tell her that her leaving him hadn't meant a thing, that he'd picked up his life and gone on without missing a beat. If it were only true . . .

Mac tossed his parka and his soaked gloves aside, then massaged the tender lump swelling on his shoulder beneath his thermal underwear and plaid flannel shirt.

"Did Paul come with you?" he asked abruptly. As he recalled, Paul Willis was a garrulous old codger, a longtime travel writer who'd been a favorite friend of Marisa's, as well as her godfather, during her teen years, when her well-to-do yachting parents had been out gallivanting around the world.

"He's in India."

"Too bad. I would have enjoyed seeing him again."

Rubbing her bruised wrist, she gave him a hostile glare. "Cut the small talk. What do you really want?"

"Answers."

"Crawl back under your rock, Mahoney. I don't owe you anything."

"Wrong. The way I see it, I've got ten years' worth of explanations coming to me. I'll settle for some straight talk about this Dr. Morris situation."

"There is no 'situation,' except in your feeble brain!" she hissed.

"Let's get one thing clear. You aren't cheating me out of an ending this time around."

Her gaze turned wary. "What do you mean?"

"I'm offering you a chance to tell your side of the story. Why else would I have tracked you to the back of beyond? A good journalist never lets a scoop slip out of his hands if he can help it, right?" His grin was cocky. "Besides, this black-market-baby story is just what I need to clinch a big contract with Independent News Network. So there's no way in hell I'm going to let you blow my chances by disappearing on me again."

"That's what this vendetta is all about? About *you?* You son of a—" With an inarticulate cry of outrage, she launched herself at him again, fingers curled into punishing claws.

Mac grunted, fending her off, and finally grabbed her wrists and twisted them behind her back so that she arched against him. "My God! What's the matter with you, woman?"

Panting, impotent, held fast against his bulk, she glared her hatred. "You have to ask? *Using* an innocent child for your own ends. You insensitive, selfish clod! Why can't you leave us alone?"

Mac tightened his hold, looking down into her eyes. "Because I always finish what I start, Marisa. Or have you forgotten?"

"Go to hell!"

He laughed. "Sorry, no can do. In case you haven't noticed, we've got ourselves a prime piece of the Polar Express roaring down outside. No one's going anywhere anytime soon, not unless they've got suicide in mind. I guess you're stuck with me."

"What? No!" Panic flickered in her eyes.

"What's the problem?" Holding both her wrists in one hand, he brushed his knuckles down her cheek. "As I recall, we once loved being alone together."

She choked. "You—"

He caught her chin in the crook of his hand, forcing her face up to his. His mouth hovered over hers, tantalizing, insulting. "Maybe you've forgotten other things, too, princess. Like how you used to sigh and moan in my arms. Like how we felt when we were a part of each other."

She trembled against him, color rolling over her cheekbones, the pulse at her temple throbbing. "Mac, no..."

"I haven't forgotten, Marisa." He bent closer, his eyes hooded. "I haven't."

"Mommy?"

Mac jerked and released her. Marisa pushed past him, going down on her knees beside the small, towheaded boy in rumpled Snoopy sweats and droopy socks. She gathered the child into her arms and pressed her flushed cheek against his, reciting a soothing litany. "Nicky, I'm sorry! Did I wake you up? Everything's all right, honey."

Wide-eyed with amazement, Nicky looked Mac over from head to heels. "Mommy, you found a cowboy!"

Mac couldn't prevent a snort. He'd been called a lot of things, but this was a new one. "Sorry, pal. I'm a city boy from New Jersey."

"You got boots." Nicky's tone was accusatory.

Mac glanced down at his old Ropers. "Yeah, well, fat lot of good they did me—my toes are frozen."

"No more than you deserve for poking your nose in where it's not wanted." Marisa scooped up Nicky and held him protectively, as fierce as a lioness defending her cub. "It's cold, Nicky. You have to get back under the covers."

As if in response to her words, a huge shudder shook Mac. "Jeez, you're right. It's as cold as the devil in here. Why haven't you got a fire going?"

She didn't answer, but her expression was mutinous. After carrying the youngster back into the den, she settled him into a nest of blankets on the sofa. Bringing up the rear, Mac noticed the pile of spent matches and scorched kindling in the fireplace, and he laughed again.

"I see your trouble. Good thing I showed up, huh, Marisa? From the looks of things, you could use some help."

"Not *yours*." Her tone was scathing.

"As they say, 'beggars can't be choosers,' princess."

She cast him a resentful look over her shoulder. "Don't call me that!"

Shrugging, Mac sat down on the edge of the stone hearth to tug off his boots and peel off his icy socks. "There's another one about 'if the shoe fits...'"

Nicky watched the exchange with sleepy-eyed interest. "What's the cowboy's name, Mommy?"

"Judas," she said. "Now go back to sleep."

"Funny name for a cowboy," Nicky mumbled, rubbing his eyes.

Mac's jaw clamped in annoyance. Fatigue and cold had made his muscles ache and his temper short. He tried to massage life back into his numb feet. "The name's Mac, kid. Your mother's been reading too many bad TV scripts."

"You call him *Mr.* Mahoney, Nicky. He's a reporter who's always had a way with words—as long as it's a cliché or a cut."

Mac blew out an exasperated breath. "Look, dammit, we can keep this up all night, or we can call a truce and make the best of it."

"Suits me, since I have nothing I want to say to you. And I'll thank you to watch your language around my son!" Nicky was curled into a ball and already snoozing again, so Marisa tucked the blankets around him, then went to the hearth and struck one match, then another. The kindling caught but died out immediately. "Damn."

"Watch your language," Mac mimicked, reaching for the box of matches. "Let me do that."

"I can take care of it!" She held on to her end of the matchbox in a small tug-of-war.

Mac lifted an eyebrow. "And I can see how well you've done so far." He saw anger play across her expressive features and pointed a warning finger at her straight nose. "Look, I'm tired, cold and hungry. You take another swing at me and I won't be responsible for what happens."

Evidently she believed him. She released the matchbox. "Fine. Go ahead. But I'd like to remind you that your circumstances are all your own doing. No one invited you here."

Busy rearranging logs and crumpling newspaper, Mac smiled dryly. "I've never let a little thing like that stop me before."

"So I've noticed."

She stared at the tiny flame that flickered, caught and began to grow under the stack of logs. Mac observed the dark smudges of fatigue—or stress—beneath her eyes. He steeled himself not to feel any sympathy. "How long has the power been off?"

"Since about noon. The phones are out and the generator won't work, either."

"No wonder it's so cold in here." He propped one bare foot on the hearth, toasting his sole before the fire's growing warmth. "When did you get here?"

"A couple of days ago."

"Must have been a hard trip, just the two of you."

She snapped her gaze from the fire's mesmerizing dance. "What is this, an interrogation?"

"Good grief, you're one suspicious female. Forget it!"

Frowning, she leaned her hands against the mantel, her knuckles white. "Forget you're the one who's unleashed a pack of lies about my husband and my son and just forced me to spread out the welcome mat for you? Not bloody likely, Mahoney! I'd love nothing better than to see the back of you right this moment."

"Tough talk, babe. But I know you're too softhearted to send me packing in the middle of a blizzard." He gave her a wolfish grin. "Not that I'd go."

She smiled back, too sweetly. "I wouldn't force a rabid dog out in weather like this, but you're another matter. So keep your distance and don't press your luck. And first thing in the morning, you're out of here, understood?"

"Sure." His assurance was meaningless.

He knew it.

She knew it.

Still, the tension in her shoulders seemed to ease a bit. Maybe she believed him. And maybe she was lying to herself the way she'd once lied to him. It would be interesting to find out.

Marisa moved away from the fire. "I'm bunking with Nicky. Find yourself a place to bed down and stay out of my way."

"I'm just beginning to defrost. I'll stay by the fire." He pushed a pair of overstuffed chairs together at the end of the sofa.

Marisa seemed ready to protest, but then her mouth compressed in annoyed resignation. "I'll find some extra blankets."

Mac pushed her to see what would happen. "And a sandwich? And some dry socks?"

She rounded on him angrily. Her eyes moved from his bare feet, up the long length of denim-covered legs to the mocking expression on his face. Whatever she saw made her swallow. "I'll see what I can do."

The corner of his mouth lifted at her concession. "Thank you."

She brushed her hand over her sleeping son's fair head, flicking Mac a suspicious look. Apparently deciding Nicky wouldn't come to any harm in Mac's presence for the moment, she picked up the lantern and left the room.

Mac's smile faded, and he let out an unsteady breath.

From the way his gut twisted just looking at her, he was still just as foolishly susceptible to Marisa Rourke as a mature thirty-year-old woman as he'd been to the lovely journalism student he'd known ten years ago. Lucky for him that now she'd declared all-out war between them.

Not that he blamed her. He hadn't exactly been comfortable with the way Jackie Horton had blindsided her on the television talk show. But Jackie and Mac's longtime producer, Tom Powell, had insisted on pinning the actress down under a cross fire of startling accusations.

"An elite baby mill..."

"Police today arrested exclusive Bel Air physician, Dr. Franco Morris..."

"*Marisa, isn't it true that you and your late husband, Victor Latimore, used Dr. Morris to acquire your own baby?*"

"*We have copies of Dr. Morris's records, verifying names, dates and fees...*"

"*It's a lie! You'll hear from my attorney!*" she shouted.

Mac grimaced at the memory. But it had to be done, for impact value, Tom had said. To pull the viewing public into the story, raise an outcry, close the baby mill. And Mac had agreed. Dr. Franco Morris had been preying on innocents long enough. Bottom line was, as always, *get the job done*.

Mac shrugged and began to unbutton his damp shirt. Every detail he unearthed was another step closer to putting the dirty doctor behind bars permanently. The involvement of a celebrity of Marisa's stature—Mac's mouth tightened in disdain at the application of such a term to a *soap opera* star—would insure that the black-market-baby investigation got the media attention it deserved. And, of course, there was the matter of that contract....

Heck, he wasn't unsympathetic! The kid was cute enough, and Marisa's maternal affection appeared genuine. Like it or not, however, Marisa Rourke Latimore had to accept responsibility for her and her dead husband's actions. And Mac should have his butt kicked for not anticipating that at the first hint of confrontation Marisa would tuck in her pretty tail and head for the hills—literally. Actions had consequences. How the hell did she think she could run away from this mess?

After spreading out his shirt on the stone hearth to dry, Mac stared into the now-blazing fire, his hands resting on the snap of his denims. He'd tackled plenty of tough assignments all over the globe—hostage crises, earthquakes, revolutions—but he knew that this one could be more than he'd bargained for, especially if he let old memories get in the way of the truth. His instincts told him those old memories were far from dead for Marisa, too. Mac hadn't missed the way her mouth trembled when he touched her. The chemistry was still there, despite everything.

Not that he wanted to fan the ashes of a dead love affair into life again. He'd learned the hard way what he could count on, what he couldn't. Still, in Mac's book, Marisa owed him. A period of enforced isolation with an old lover hadn't been in his game plan when he'd discovered her involvement in the Morris story, but he was human enough to take advantage of the present situation. He would enjoy seeing that she finally paid—at least in some small measure—for the way she'd betrayed him so long ago.

His smile returned at the prospect. He unfastened his jeans, then slid out of them and draped them over a chair back. They began to steam almost immediately. Clad in long-sleeved thermal undershirt and long johns, he rested both hands on the mantel, letting the waves of heat soak into him. The frantic detective work and two-day drive in stinking weather, not to mention that mile hike uphill in a snowstorm, were catching up with him, and the warmth was making him drowsy.

"Here, this is the only thing I could—" Behind him, Marisa's words broke off with a small gasp of outrage.

Mac straightened, stretched and gave her a lazy glance over his shoulder. "Get a grip, princess. You've seen me in my skivvies before."

"Not an experience I wanted to repeat," she snapped. Face flaming, she dropped blankets, a rolled-up pair of wool socks and a paper plate holding a ham sandwich into a pile beside the chairs he'd chosen. "But I suppose your behaving with the least bit of common decency is too much to expect."

"Hey, I was wet. You want me to sleep in damp clothes and catch my death?"

"It's a thought." Without looking at him, she kicked off her shoes and crawled onto the sofa beside her son, arranging the blankets over them both.

Mac wrapped himself in a fluffy comforter and sat in the chair to pull on the dry socks. He made his tone conversational. "You know, the most sensible thing would be for us to cuddle together to conserve body heat."

"In your dreams, Mahoney." Her voice was muffled by the piles of blankets, but the agitation in her tone was plain. "Shut up so we can sleep."

Reaching for the sandwich, Mac propped his long legs in the seat of the matching chair. *Yeah, in my dreams,* he thought. *If she only knew.*

Halfway through the sandwich, he paused long enough to examine it more closely. Ham, cheese, mustard, no mayo. He hated mayonnaise. She'd remembered....

The next mouthful went down hard. She remembered. As much as he did? With as much pain? They'd had so much. At least *he'd* thought they had. Did she regret at all that she'd left him without a word?

Mac set aside the unfinished sandwich, huddling down in the chair and pulling the comforter up around his ears. Dancing orange shadows illuminated the room and the rounded forms of the woman and child on the big sofa. Although the cadence of her breathing was even, he knew she wasn't asleep.

"Marisa?" His voice was low, barely audible above the howling of the unrelenting storm outside.

"Hmm?"

"Where did it go wrong?"

There was a long silence, so long that Mac decided she wasn't going to answer him.

Finally, she replied. "Does it matter?"

Mac had no answer that he could voice, but it did matter. *God help him. It did.*

Two

——

Marisa awoke smiling, her dreams melting into gossamer images of beaches and a green-eyed man and the sensation of sunshine warming her skin. She stretched, indulging in the perfect euphoric moment. In the next instant, sleep slipped completely away, and she sat up with a gasp.

Nicky! The space on the sofa beside her was empty. Blood surging, Marisa threw back the blankets and rolled to her feet in a panic.

Above the crackle of the steadily burning fire, high-pitched childish chatter drifted from the direction of the kitchen. She stumbled toward the rear of the lodge, stopping short at the cased opening into the cozy dining area and country kitchen.

"My mommy can do that better."

"Yeah, kid? Well, your mommy's still snoozing like Goldilocks, so I guess it's up to me. See if this suits you."

Marisa quit breathing. Mac Mahoney stood with his back to her—his *bare,* beautifully muscled back—pushing a glass of orange juice across the counter to Nicky. Her mouth went dry. Mac's shoulders were as broad as ever, the well-defined muscles covered by bronzed skin. Her fingers tingled with the urge to explore the velvety texture.

The dim natural light filtering into the kitchen revealed spoons, pitchers and puddles of sticky orange concentrate littering the dividing bar. Outside, the wind continued to howl and the sky, still a sullen lead color, filled the air with flurries of gray snow, but the lodge was noticeably warmer, thanks to Mac. Yet the image of him stoking the fire during the night while she slept unsettled her. So did the realization that a pair of snug jeans on the right man could be utterly devastating to the female libido.

"Don't like 'The Three Bears.'" Nicky perched on a tall stool, slurping juice from a tumbler. "Too sissy."

Mac poured bottled water into a battered percolator and rummaged in the cabinets for coffee. "You never heard the real story then."

"What story?"

"Not the one they tell babies." Mac frowned over the measuring scoop and read the side of the red coffee can again. "The one about how the bear family gobbled up Goldilocks for breakfast instead of porridge. Fricasseed blonde."

"Really? Cool."

"The twit got what she deserved for breaking and entering, so let that be a lesson to you, kid. There aren't any free lunches in this world."

"Mommy makes my lunches. And she puts four scoops of that stuff in the coffeepot. Are you sure you're not a cowboy?"

Marisa couldn't resist a smile at that. Mac surreptitiously unscooped a couple of spoonfuls of coffee grounds out of the strainer basket with his fingers, then turned on the gas burner of the bottled-propane stove. Marisa couldn't help noticing how his thick, mahogany-colored hair grew long at his nape. He'd always been too impatient for regular haircuts.

"Sorry," he said to the boy. "I wouldn't know the north end of a horse from the south."

"That's what I was afraid of." Nicky sighed, then his blue eyes brightened. "Are you the new daddy I asked Santa to bring?"

"Nicky!" Marisa nearly swallowed her tongue in chagrin. Face flaming, she stepped into the kitchen to quiet her all-too-outspoken offspring. Mac turned toward her, and she drew up sharply with a horrified gasp. "Oh, my God."

A painful-looking blue-and-purple streak ran from the top of Mac's muscled shoulder to his collarbone—her doing. That blow with the poker had done more damage than she'd realized. Remorse flooded her.

"Mac, I'm so sorry!" Without thinking, she lifted her hand, hovered hesitantly over the livid bruise for a moment, then gently stroked the area of abused flesh as if to draw out the pain.

The instant she touched him, Mac shuddered. Swift as a striking snake, he captured her wrist, holding her in midstroke, her fingers barely brushing his skin. His lips compressed, and something emerald and potent and wild flared behind his eyes in a look so heated Marisa felt dazed and dizzy.

"Don't do that again—unless you're prepared for the consequences." His voice was rough, his lean jaw shadowed by dark stubble. He looked like a pirate, ruthlessly masculine and intent on plunder.

Marisa blinked, unnerved and confused. Her breathing came short and choppy, and her skin felt unnaturally sensitized. Mac's fingers were like a fiery bracelet burning into her wrist, tracking the pulse that thundered there. Was he merely warning her against trying to wallop him again, or was that dangerous golden glint in his green eyes the product of something else? Something as elemental as the arc of electricity that had passed through them both at her innocent touch. Thoroughly rattled, Marisa twisted her hand free and stepped back in haste.

"No. Of course. That is—" Realizing she was babbling, she shoved her disheveled hair from her face and drew a deep breath. "No, I won't. You should put ice on it. Or maybe a hot pack? There's bound to be some liniment..."

Their contact broken, Mac was once again his usual mocking self. Half-smiling, he gave an easy shrug, as if that disturbing moment had been only in Marisa's imagination. "Relax, princess. I've had worse."

"Oh. Yeah, right."

A shiver ran down Marisa's spine at his casual acceptance of the dangers inherent in his work. Over the years, it had been hard for her to miss Mac's news reports from hot spots all over the globe. Not that she'd been looking for him on purpose, of course. It was just that any time there was a political crisis, a natural disaster or another injustice to be revealed to the world, the viewing public could count on Mac Mahoney reporting from the thick of things. In his dedication and passionate pursuit of truth, Mac had never let a little thing like personal safety stand in the way of a good story.

"Just don't let it happen again." Mac's voice was gruff as he turned back to the stove. "Coffee will be ready in a minute."

"Yes. Uh, thanks." Weakly, Marisa took the stool next to Nicky's and gave the boy a good-morning hug. Thankfully the lad hadn't noticed anything out of the ordinary about his mother's reaction to their visitor. "How're you doing, partner?"

"Call me Tex today, Mommy."

"All right, Tex. Was your bedroll comfortable last night?"

"Yup." Nicky grinned, his face shining with impish pleasure at the imaginary role. "Me and Mac got up with the roosters. Didn't we, Mac?"

Mac grunted something unintelligible.

"That's Mr. Mahoney, Tex," she corrected.

"Leave it," Mac ordered. "We don't need that kind of formality. Right, Tex?"

"Right, Mac!"

Marisa would have argued, but then Mac shoved a mug of black-as-sin coffee at her, automatically pushing the sugar and dry creamer in her direction. "Thanks." Marisa swallowed hard around a sudden thickness in her throat.

After all this time, he still remembered how she liked her morning coffee. A little thing, but the realization touched some chord deep inside her, softening her wariness and hostility— Marisa reined in this new feeling with a firm hand. This was treacherous territory. She couldn't afford to let down her guard, not with Nicky's future at stake!

And what had Nicky meant about a "new daddy"? Had her little boy been pining for a male role model without her even being aware of it? she wondered guiltily. Being a single parent wasn't easy, but she'd done her best since Victor's death. However, for Nicky misguidedly to settle his affections on a cynical, hard-nosed reporter who was intent on ruining their lives would be pure disaster! Yes, the sooner

Mac Mahoney was on his way and out of her life again, the better.

Stirring her coffee, she flicked Mac a brief glance. His bronze nipples pebbled in the cool air, winking from a light thatching of brown hair that tapered down the corrugated muscles of a belly just as flat and hard at thirty-seven as it had been a decade earlier. Swallowing, she dragged her gaze away. "Ah, I suppose you'll want to make an early start...."

One dark eyebrow lifted, and the edges of his hard mouth curved upward in a pitying smile. "Never give up, do you, princess?"

Her chin tilted in preparation for battle. "I thought I'd made myself clear—"

"So has the weatherman." Mac tapped an index finger on the small, battery-operated weather-band radio sitting on the counter. "Good thing Paul keeps his pantries well stocked. Time to batten down the hatches."

Marisa's fingers clenched around the handle of the mug. "Wh-what does that mean?"

"Travelers warnings are everywhere, all roads are closed and nothing's moving in or out of these mountains. They say we've got three or four more days of this at least. Might let up by Christmas Eve, earliest."

"A white Christmas? Oh, boy!" Nicky crowed. "I never had snow for Christmas before! Is the chimney big enough for Santa? I better go look!"

He scrambled off the stool and raced into the den. Dismayed, Marisa stared after him. Trapped up here with Mac Mahoney, forced to endure his accusations, his cross-examinations and her own wayward responses every time he came too near—for Christmas? It was too much to contemplate! Fuming, she glared at him. "I'm not staying here with you. If you won't leave, I will!"

"Don't be a fool, Marisa. The roads are treacherous. You wouldn't get ten feet."

She knew she was being unreasonable, fighting the inevitable, but her mouth was mulish. "I might. And at least I wouldn't have to endure your odious company!"

"You can't fool me. You might risk your own neck—and I'd be happy to let you, believe me—but you'd never risk the kid's."

Her shoulders slumped. "No."

"That's what I thought."

The smugness of his expression made her long to smack it off his face. But violence wasn't the answer, so to restrain the impulse she lifted her mug to take a fortifying sip. The bitterness of the double-strength brew made her choke.

"Too strong?" Mac asked mildly.

Marisa climbed off the stool and emptied her mug in the sink. She followed with the entire pot of coffee. "Everything about you comes on too strong."

"Yeah, too bad you're stuck with me, huh?"

She bit her lip, frustration and helplessness choking her.

All right, she thought, she had to accept the situation, uncomfortable as it made her—but that didn't mean she had to like it. Nor did it mean she had to give Mac any answers just because circumstances forced them together. She had better sense than to let outdated emotions cloud the fact that his actions had made him her enemy now. There were larger issues at stake—keeping warm and fed on top of the list.

Yes, that was the ticket. Stay cool but civil, wait out the storm and make certain she gave Mac Mahoney *nothing* that he could use in his damned story! He'd eventually get bored and move on to seek other prey.

"Since you barged in without an invitation, you'll have to earn your keep, Mahoney. Get dressed, for God's sake. We need more wood inside, buckets of snow to melt for washing and flushing. I won't have any freeloaders, is that clear?"

"I can do my part." He raised his eyebrows. "You intend to feed me breakfast before I brave the storm?"

Belligerence gave her voice an edge. "What do you want?"

Mac bared his teeth—a peculiar, predatory smile that made the hair on the back of Marisa's neck stand up. "Porridge?"

He got oatmeal. A bowl of oatmeal sporting a happy face made with a jelly smile and two raisins for eyes. Nicky, dressed in corduroys, sweater and six-guns, had insisted. "You're bigger than me. You must get hungrier."

The boy's bright blue eyes looked so expectant, Mac didn't have the heart to tell him that he despised oatmeal, no matter how artfully it was decorated. Grimly, Mac pushed back the cuffs of his plaid flannel shirt and picked up his spoon. It couldn't be any worse than Bedouin goat-milk couscous.

Marisa, her face freshly scrubbed and hair pulled back in a ponytail, but still wearing the slacks and sweater she'd slept in, set another bowl before Nicky and ruffled his fair hair affectionately. "Eat up. Cowboys need their energy."

Trained to observe, Mac noted the easy manner between mother and son. It didn't jibe with the picture of the affluent "star" foisting the upbringing of her child on paid servants, only seeing the little tyke when he was paraded before the dinner guests. Instead, they shared a rapport that could only have been built with genuine love and hands-on diligence.

Marisa had help, of course. When he'd gone to the pseudo-Spanish Beverly Hills monstrosity Victor Latimore had built for his new bride, intent on offering Marisa a chance to say her piece about the Morris matter, Mac had met Gwen Olsen, Marisa's nanny-housekeeper. Pulling the truth out of Gwen that Marisa had vanished without leaving so much as a note behind had produced a powerful feeling of déjà vu, launching Mac into the chase that had led him here, straight to a damned bowl of oatmeal!

Grimacing, he shoveled in the first mouthful. To his surprise, it wasn't half-bad. She'd laced it with brown sugar and a touch of cinnamon.

Nicky grinned up at him. "Good, huh?"

Mac tried another bite, decided the kid was right and dug in. Maybe if his own mother had possessed the imagination to draw faces in his cereal bowl, he wouldn't have grown up so wild and rebellious.

But Vivian Mahoney, abandoned by her husband and beaten down by life and the two menial jobs she worked merely to keep herself and her son fed, hadn't had the time for such niceties or the energy to cope with her street-smart son. In fact, if it hadn't been for the coach down at the local Boys' Club and a stint in the Golden Gloves boxing circuit, no telling what kind of turn—for the worse—Mac's life might have taken. His mother had died when he was seventeen, and he'd always thought she had not so much given up on life as simply been worn out. But growing up on the mean streets had given Mac his drive, propelling him through Princeton on a scholarship while he worked double shifts and weekends at a foundry. When you'd never had much of anything, you took nothing for granted.

Especially not a woman's love.

Marisa was finishing her own bowl of hot cereal, her gaze abstracted as she poked into cupboards and a pantry, pulling out various cans. Face bare and hair scraped back, she hardly looked like a glamorous actress, but her classic Ingrid Bergman-type bone structure gave her a compelling beauty that would remain ageless. Mac wondered what millionaire Victor Latimore had seen when he looked at his wife.

"I think I'll put together a stew to simmer over the fireplace for our lunch. How's that sound, Nicky?" she asked.

"Can I help pour things into the pot?"

"Sure, honey." She was already pulling a hefty cast-iron kettle from the cupboard.

Mac pushed back his empty bowl. "Where'd you learn to cook? I didn't think that was something you 'Lifestyles of the Rich and Famous' types did."

Her look was level. "I guess there's a lot of things you don't know."

Annoyance hardened his mouth. If there was one thing Mac didn't stand for, it was being accused of not having his facts down cold. "What I don't know, I find out. That's a promise." He slid off the kitchen stool, gratified by the shimmer of apprehension clouding her blue eyes. "I'll go get that wood."

Sometime later, Mac finished stacking firewood from the backyard pile onto the porch near the back door, then gratefully carried a final armload inside to the hearth in the den. Visibility was nearly zero, and even the short trek between the lodge and its various outbuildings and sheds was an arduous one given the grueling wind-driven snow. Paul had a considerable stockpile of firewood, but if the storm kept up as predicted and power remained out, Mac thought he might eventually have to take the ax he'd found in the toolshed to a couple of the trees surrounding the place. Not a prospect he relished, considering the weather.

"Hold it right there, you varmint!" A pint-size *bandito* brandishing twin cap pistols and wearing a bandanna over his nose leapt out from behind a fort of pillows and blankets draped over chair backs.

"Don't shoot, Tex. I'm one of the good guys."

"That's what they all say, partner. Now reach for the sky."

Mac's lips twitched as he dumped the wood on the hearth. "Bloodthirsty galoot, aren't you?"

"I ain't no galoot—I'm a cowboy!" Pulling down his kerchief, Nicky gave Mac an indignant look.

Unfastening his parka, Mac added sticks to the fire and punched it up. "I'd never have guessed."

"Well . . . well, *shoot!*" Disgusted, Nicky plopped down on the sofa arm. "Bet if I had a horse you could tell. I hope Santa brings me one. Think he will?"

That stopped Mac. "Uh, hard to say. Where's your mother? Upstairs?"

"Nah." Nicky rolled onto his back and began to drum his heels on the sofa. "Outside. She made me stay here. What does 'hold down the fort' mean, anyway?"

"What the hell!" An image of Marisa frozen in a snow-bank flashed through Mac's head. The vision was at once ludicrous, startling and scary. "Outside? Where?"

"Checking the gen-gena—"

"Generator?"

"Yeah. And you'd better not let Mommy hear that bad word. She'll make you sit in the time-out chair."

"*She* won't be able to sit when I get through with her!" Muttering darkly, Mac jerked at his parka zipper. "Damn fool woman—what's she thinking?"

Halfway across the den, he turned abruptly and pointed a finger at Nicky. "You stay put until I get back. Sheriff's orders. Okay, Tex?"

Nicky's eyes were wide. "Yes, sir. Can I be your deputy?"

"You got it, kid."

The boy's awed and triumphant voice followed Mac out the door. "I *knew* he was a cowboy."

The wind hit Mac smack in the face and took his breath away. Leaning against it, he came down the porch steps, ducked his head and slogged through the growing drifts toward the small lean-to attached to the combination barn and garage set behind the lodge proper. From the power lines strung from it, he guessed it was the location of the generator. On a clear day, there would be a commanding view of the snow-topped Sierra Nevada peaks in the distance, but now everything was just a gray white blankness, the silhouettes of the buildings barely visible and the outline of Marisa's tracks already disappearing.

The wind buffeted Mac's shoulders, and ice particles stung his cheeks. Marisa was so slender, just a puff at this force could send her tumbling down the mountainside—and then what? That she would be stupid enough to place herself—and therefore the kid—in danger incensed him. He burst through the door of the lean-to in a rage. "What the hell do you think you're doing?"

Marisa jumped and dropped the flashlight with which she'd been inspecting the gasoline-powered generator. The beam went out when it hit the concrete floor, and the little room was plunged into almost total gloom. "Now look what you've made me do!" Falling to her hands and knees, she groped for the flashlight. Clad in a puffy down jacket, knitted cap and gloves, she looked as young and delectable as any ski-resort snow bunny. Then she found the flashlight, flicked it on and speared him right in the eyes with the bright beam. "At least close the damn door."

He kicked it shut, but the violence did little to relieve the pressure that was building up inside. "Just what the devil are you doing?" he roared.

Her chin came up. "Giving this thing another look. You got a problem with that?"

"You're damn right I do!" He stepped closer, grabbed her arm and shook her, making the flashlight beam bounce. "From now on, don't you poke that pretty nose of yours outside without telling me first. Is that clear?"

"I don't take orders from you, Mahoney."

"Don't let that ridiculous stiff-necked pride of yours get you in trouble. This isn't the kind of weather you can play around in."

"I wasn't playing. I was trying to help!"

"Then use your head. Unless all that daytime drivel you've been feeding the viewing public has left it totally empty."

Her teeth snapped together. "Keep your contempt for my profession to yourself."

"Now there's a trick and a half! Last time I had the misfortune to tune in, you and that pretty boy you play against were cuddled up in a hot under-the-covers scene. Tell me, do you often work naked in this 'profession' of yours?"

Marisa's eyes flashed her annoyance. "Dear Mac. As abrasive and crude as ever."

"I'm paid to ask the hard questions, honey," he drawled.

"Eric and I share a great respect for each other's work. It's a matter of trust and communication." Her voice went sugar sweet. "But some people have trouble understanding such a simple, basic concept. And, unlike others I can name, Eric has never made so much as a single off-color remark to me."

"Too tongue-tied by your beauty au naturel, I guess."

"For your information, Eric and I have never gotten naked together... *on camera*." Smiling as he chewed on that, Marisa pointed at the generator. "Now, why don't you use

a little of that brute strength you're so fond of showing off
to crank this thing!''

Jaw taut, Mac glared at her, then reached for the starter
rope. Ten frustrating minutes later, he gave up. "It's no use.
If I could break it down, maybe clean out the carbure-
tor..."

Marisa sighed. "Forget it then. We'll just have to make
do.''

"Not something a princess is accustomed to, eh?"

She looked blank for a moment, then pitched the flashlight at his head and stormed out of the lean-to. Mac ducked
and went after her, his temper at the flash point. He caught
up with her in two steps, looped his arm around her waist
and physically dragged her into the garage, ignoring her futile attempts to break free as the wind howled around them.

"Let me go!"

Shutting the garage door behind them, Mac obliged,
thrusting her down onto a pile of stacked boxes. "Sit. And
shut up. We're going to get a few things straight."

"I'm sick of you!" Marisa whipped off her cap, shook
her hair free and wiped her damp face. "Sick of the sight of
you, do you hear?"

"Yeah. You're my favorite person, too."

Mac looked around. The garage was frigid, but being out
of the wind was a relief. Several generations of tarps and
tools and outdated farm and sporting equipment of every
description hung from the rafters and walls. A gray sedan
sat in one of the parking spaces, the vehicle Marisa had used
on her escape from Los Angeles. Which brought him back
to the reason he was here.

"Are you ready to tell me what really went down with you
and your husband and Dr. Morris?"

Marisa spluttered in fury. "Nothing, I told you! I never
heard of him until that day in Jackie Horton's studio!

Nicky's adoption was handled by the Latimore Corporation attorneys, and it was all perfectly legal, Mr. Hotshot Reporter!''

Mac's voice was quiet. "Then why did you run?"

"I did not—" She caught a shaky breath.

"This place wasn't as far as you planned to go with the kid, was it? What were you thinking? Canada, maybe? Some Greek Island? Talk about parental kidnapping with a twist, jet-set-style."

Hot color burned her cheeks, but she looked him in the eye and denied it. "Assumptions, Mahoney. You've got no facts, and no self-respecting journalist is going to run a story based merely on air. You used to be capable of better than this."

"You'd do anything to protect the kid, wouldn't you?"

"He's my *son*. What do you think?"

"I think there's a birth mother out there who's owed some explanations."

"Look, I feel for the women this Dr. Morris exploited, but that's only one side of this story. There are families involved, families and lives that you're disrupting, even destroying—hasn't that occurred to you?"

"We find the truth, we get justice. It's as simple as that."

"God, it's not!" She stood up, staring at him in sheer disbelief. "Why must it always be either black or white with you, Mac? The world has shades of gray, too."

"All I want to do is shut down the baby mill."

"At what cost?" she cried. "Do the ends always justify the means to you?"

"If it keeps the bastard from using other innocent women like he did the kid's mother."

"*I'm* his mother! And I'm just as innocent and undeserving of this mess that you've made of our lives! Can't you for one minute see past your damned story to realize that?"

"The facts say otherwise. And you're going to have to face up to them eventually, one way or the other."

"I've told you, your facts are all wrong!" Marisa shoved him hard in the chest with both hands. "And the *kid's* name is Nicholas!"

He nodded, barely rocked by her puny blow. "As in the saint, right? Which reminds me. You've got a problem. He thinks Santa Claus is bringing him a horse for Christmas."

"A horse. For Christmas? That's just—" she gulped "—four days?"

Mac nodded again.

Her expression was stricken with a horrible realization. "Oh, God. We won't be able to drive out by then."

He shook his head.

"Everything's at home. All Nicky's presents. I had everything on his list. I can't even get to a store! I never thought...I never dreamed..." Feeling behind her, she sat down heavily on the boxes again. Her eyes filled. "Oh, no."

Mac felt something hit him in the gut. "Hey, don't do that."

She wasn't listening. A tear splashed over her lashes and trailed down her cheek. "He's just a baby. He'll be so disappointed. How will I explain?"

Mac was gruff. "You'll think of something."

"It's all your fault." Her eyes were indigo, swimming in liquid crystal. "If you hadn't started this, he'd be safe at home where he belongs, sleeping in his own bed, waiting for Christmas morning. I'll never forgive you for this, Mahoney."

"Marisa..." He was beside her, cradling her tear-streaked face in his gloved palms, bending forward so that his forehead almost touched hers. His throat felt thick. "Lord, help me, you're still such a baby yourself."

"Because I believe in dreams, Mac?" She held on to his wrists, looking up at him in misery. "You never really understood, did you? You were always too much the cynic to realize that dreams are the most important things in life. Especially a little boy's Christmas dreams."

From deep in his memory came a vivid picture of a small dark-haired lad—Mac, himself—with his nose pressed to a store window, longing with every fiber of his six-year-old being for the magnificent red dragline with the Tonka name on its side. It was better than a dinosaur, better than a fire truck, and most certainly better than the pair of sturdy school shoes that had been the only present to appear that long-ago Christmas morning.

Mac swallowed. "That's not true."

Her lids dropped and more tears slid down her face. "What am I going to do?"

"Marisa, don't." Seeking to comfort, he nuzzled her temple, then the corner of her eye, tasted the salty essence, murmured soothing nonsense. Like a flower turning to face the sun, she raised her face to his. Mac's gloved thumb caught at the corner of her mouth. Slowly her eyes opened and she searched his expression, wondering and wary. She did not pull away from his touch. "You're trembling," Mac said.

"It—it's cold."

"I know." He looked at her mouth and groaned. "It's been winter forever." He couldn't help himself. He had to see if her mouth was still the flavor of honey and spice. Lowering his lips to hers, he kissed her.

She tasted even better than he'd remembered—a lush, soft sweetness, intoxicating, addicting. Mac sensed the little sighing breath she gave and opened his mouth to inhale it, to breathe *her*. Her hands tightened on his wrists. Forgetting himself, the past, the cold, he drew his tongue along the seam of her lips and was rewarded when they parted. Deepening the kiss, he drank deep of her, making love to her with just his mouth until neither of them could bear any more and they drew apart.

Mac dropped his hands and stepped back. Dazed, Marisa touched her lips, and he watched as the light in her eyes faded and changed into a look of dismay. "That shouldn't have happened," she said, her voice unsteady.

"No." Mac felt as stunned and rocky as she looked.

For a moment, neither of them could say anything else. Then Marisa stood and moved toward the door, brushing non-existent dust from her slacks. "I've got to get back to Nicky."

"Marisa, wait." He cleared his throat. "Uh, about this Christmas thing ... I've been thinking."

She hesitated. "Yes?"

"We're two reasonably intelligent, imaginative people. Surely somewhere around this place we can come up with a treasure or two that would please your little cowpoke come Christmas morning—until you can get to the store-bought stuff."

"Like what?"

"Well..." Scanning the dim interior, Mac spotted a likely item and hauled it down. "How about this sled? I could fix the runner, splash a little paint on it—there's bound to be some paint around. And what would be more perfect for his first white Christmas?"

"You—you'd do that?"

"Sure." He set the rickety sled aside. "And you were always pretty good with a needle. Maybe you could whip something up that would appeal to him."

She paused before the garage door, chewing her lip, a small frown pleating her brow. "Yes, I could do that."

"Hey, we'll cut a tree, string popcorn. It'll be straight out of Norman Rockwell."

Marisa gave a shaky smile, bemused by the picture he was painting. "It's a solution, but this doesn't seem quite up your alley, Mahoney. What's the catch?"

On the point of pushing open the door, Mac sobered. He was amazing himself with this cracked idea, but what the hell! He did feel partly responsible for ruining Nicky's Christmas. And there was that memory of the Tonka dragline. Slowly he offered Marisa his hand. "No catch. Just a Christmas cease-fire. For the kid's sake."

She studied his face for a long moment, her expression mingling distrust, uncertainty and hope. Then, wordlessly, she placed her hand in his. Squeezing her fingers, Mac pulled her into the shelter of his body, and they prepared to cross the stormy, snowswept wasteland together.

Three

Mac sprawled on the sofa, full of Marisa's tasty stew and pleasantly tired from splitting firewood. The unfamiliar sensation of peace and a strange contentment made his eyelids droop as he inspected the pair seated cross-legged in front of the hearth. Their fair heads bent over their work, Marisa and Nicky sat surrounded by a growing mountain of colorful paper chains. The Christmas cease-fire—fought to a diplomatic solution within the confines of a frigid garage only hours ago—appeared in full force. Mac wondered how long it would last.

"This'll be just like the pioneers' Christmas trees, huh, Mommy?"

Busy with tape and scissors, Marisa nodded. "Absolutely. Homemade decorations are really the prettiest. And we can string some popcorn and bake sugar cookies to hang, too."

"Are we really going to cut down our tree right out of the woods, Mac?"

"Sure thing, Tex."

Bobbing to his feet, Nicky leaned on the sofa arm, his eyes bright with eagerness. "When? Now?"

Mac chuckled. "Could we wait until the wind dies down a bit? I just got warm again."

"You're a good chopper. Mommy said so."

"It's nice to be appreciated." Mac's tone was dry. His gaze caressed the supple curve of Marisa's back, and she stiffened as though he'd actually touched her under her sweater.

"We've got lots to do before we're ready for the actual tree, Nicky," she said, rising with a rainbow of paper chains in her arms. She wouldn't meet Mac's eyes. "I'll put these up and get started on that cookie dough, okay?"

"Can Mac help us make 'em?"

She hesitated, looking back over her shoulder, then shrugged. "Sure. If he wants."

As Marisa disappeared into the kitchen, Nicky fixed Mac with his bright blue gaze. "You ever made cookies?"

"Not that I recall," Mac admitted. Cookie baking had not been high on his mother's list of priorities.

Laying his small hand on Mac's muscular forearm, Nicky said kindly, "Don't worry, it's easy. I'll help you."

Deep down in a place Mac hadn't realized still existed, something melted at the boy's generous spirit. Small wonder Marisa was so proud of the kid. Mac tousled Nicky's hair. "Thanks, partner. I'll count on it."

"Mac..." Nicky chewed his lip, looking uncertain.

Cocking an eyebrow, Mac gathered the boy to his side. "Something eating you, cowpoke?"

"Mommy 'splained about getting stuck in the snow, and how Santa Claus might have trouble finding us and all, and that's okay—I'm a big boy—but..."

"But what?"

"But I forgot the Christmas present Gwen helped me pick out at home, and now I don't have *nothing* to give Mommy!" Nicky finished in a rush.

"She'll understand—"

"No, I gotta give her a present. I gotta!"

Feeling helpless, Mac lifted the agitated child onto his lap and tried to soothe him. "Well, we'll just have to think about that, won't we?"

"I've thought and thought," Nicky said in a mournful voice. "I could build her a box to keep things in, but she won't let me have a hammer."

"Smart mommy," Mac muttered. But Nicky looked so doleful Mac knew he couldn't let it go at that. "I wonder...does she still like fancy earrings?"

"Uh-huh. How'd you know?"

Mac shifted uncomfortably. "I, uh, your mom and I were good friends a long time ago. First time I saw her, she was wearing these weird earrings that looked like giant comets."

"Now she's even got some that have snakes on them! They're cool."

Mac looked down into the boy's expectant face. "That's the answer then. I saw some fine wire out in the garage. We'll make some hooks and then glue something interesting on them like feathers or baby pinecones. We'll keep it a secret and she'll really be surprised."

A skeptical frown pleated Nicky's brow. "I don't know."

"Trust me, she'll love them. Especially if they come from you."

Satisfied, Nicky settled more comfortably against Mac's chest, prattling on about what odds and ends he might find for the planned earrings. Mac hardly heard him. His own unthinking reassurance had caused something painful to resonate in his memory and the past rose to taunt him.

The beach had been their magic place in those early days, where they basked in the sun, the gulls crying overhead, and felt the cool silk of the water and the harsh grit of the warm sand against their bodies. And he was teasing her, laughing at her mock complaints.

"I hate my mouth," she'd said.

"I love your mouth."

"It's too big."

"It's just right."

"My nose is too small."

"Your nose is perfect."

"And my eyes . . ."

He'd growled, "What about your gorgeous eyes?"

"They're just plain old blue!"

"And you're plainly fishing for a compliment! So why don't you try catching this instead?"

He'd tossed the box into her lap and flopped down on the towel beside her, an arm thrown over his face to show how unconcerned he was. But it was a sham, for he'd been tense with expectancy and doing his damnedest not to show it.

"What is it?" she asked, dusting sand from her legs.

"Open it and see."

He heard her peeling away the brown paper wrapping and her swift indrawn breath. "Oh, Mac, they're lovely."

Taking a chance, he glanced at the dainty set of earrings made from a pair of Bolivian pesos left over from his last foreign assignment, and then up into her face. The pleasure he saw reflected there made him relax again. "Yeah, well, I owed you, right? For making you lose that earring the other night."

She blushed at the reminder of the passionate encounter that had left them both breathless and her minus a lot more than mere jewelry. And they never found the missing earring, even though he searched the interior of his old Buick for a long time. But she was fair. "That wasn't all your fault. Besides, I lose them all the time!"

He rose up on an elbow, squinting up at her, his belly tightening at the sight of her slenderness in her minuscule bikini. "Well, they're nothing much—"

Marisa touched his mouth with her index finger to silence his excuses. He was sensitive about her affluent background and the fact that his mother had raised him alone on just a waitress's earnings. And a struggling reporter's salary—even if he'd landed a teaching position for a semester—didn't run to expensive gifts. He was casually offhand because down deep he feared she'd find him somehow lacking, that a girl who'd had all of wealth's advantages would realize she had made a terrible mistake falling for a guy from his street-tough background. But he underestimated her intuitive understanding of him.

"I love them. Especially since they come from you." She bent and pressed a quick kiss to his mouth. "Thank you."

"You don't have to wear them in public or anything—"

"Will you stop? They're perfect!" Laughter bubbled from her throat. "And only an uncouth lout would criticize his own gift!"

Faster than a thought, Mac caught her wrists and rolled her onto her back, their legs tangling. "A lout, am I? Those are fighting words where I come from, lady!"

Lowering her lashes, she gave him a sultry smile. "You're not so tough."

"No?" Desire blazed at her challenge.

Marisa reached up to pull his head down. "No."

And then Mac was kissing her, kisses salty sweet and wonderful, teaching her about herself and him, about what loving a man truly meant. They'd had so many dreams then. Damp and replete from their loving, they'd talked about them, whispering secrets in the warm California nights, then turning to each other again, so hungry, so eager to fill each other, even though in the end their dreams hadn't been the same at all....

"I'll take him now, Mac. Mac?"

He jumped at the sound of Marisa's soft voice, and looked up into the azure depths of her eyes to find past and present mingling in an instant of confused arousal. Then reality returned, and she was there, reaching not for her lover, but for her son, who'd fallen sound asleep against Mac's flannel-covered chest. "Leave him," Mac said, his tone gruff. "He's not hurting anything."

"I can take him." Though still soft, her voice took on a defensive edge. "Besides, I'm sure you aren't comfortable."

Bending, she scooped Nicky into her arms. Her hair brushed Mac's cheek, and her scent, flowery and female, enveloped him. His body leapt in response, but she was already turning away to settle Nicky into a nest of blankets near the hearth to finish his nap.

Mac rose and made a job of poking at the fire, piling in new logs—anything to spare himself the embarrassment of her noticing how easily she could stir him. His involuntary response angered him. Remembered kisses were eternally golden because they were the ideal, he told himself, explaining away the moment of weakness, ignoring the fact that the kiss they'd shared that morning outshone even that unforgettable ideal like a star gone nova beside a sputtering candle.

Putting down the poker, Mac frowned into the flames, his mouth set. Marisa was dangerous, all right, and he'd better not forget it. He had learned the hard way once before, and Mac Mahoney had no intention of getting burned again, especially at the expense of the story of his career. He hadn't missed the frightened light in Marisa's eyes when she found him holding her son. No matter what they had shared in the past, she still saw Mac as a threat. And *that* told him she was hiding something.

Truce or not, sooner or later he'd find out what.

It wasn't until the next afternoon that the storm died down enough for a Christmas tree-hunting expedition, but by that time Marisa's nerves were so overstretched she was ready to scream. Cabin fever took on a whole new meaning when she was forced to spend it in close company with a man who despised her.

Marisa paused on the trail Mac's boots had cut through the snow and raised hands high over her head to take a deep cleansing breath of the icy air. Leaden clouds lay low over the distant peaks, and the wind was already picking up again with the promise of more dangerous weather within the hour. In his hooded parka and with an ax slung over his broad shoulder, Mac plowed a path through the drifts toward a thicket of young firs, followed by Nicky, who looked round as a barrel in his bright red ski jacket and knit cap.

Stretching again, Marisa welcomed the fresh air and physical exertion. Maybe if she was tired enough, she could sleep tonight instead of listening to the sound of a man's quiet breathing into the wee hours of the night. To save his back, Mac had dragged a mattress down from an upstairs bedroom rather than spend another night stretched between two chairs, but he'd laid it between the sofa and hearth, so near that she could have easily touched him in her sleep. It was a temptation she couldn't afford, especially after the way he'd kissed her.

Marisa raised her gloved fingers to her red cheeks, spanked to bright color by the cold and the memory of her reaction to Mac's mouth on hers. All he'd had to do was touch her, and she was lost in the heat of old magic. She stifled a groan. What kind of a fool did that make her?

At least when their hostility was out in the open, she stood a chance of keeping her distance. Being civil, even as stilted as this so-called truce was, put them much too close for her peace of mind. She tried to keep busy with the various chores of survival and stitching one of Uncle Paul's old socks into a stick horse, complete with yarn mane and button eyes, for Nicky's Christmas. But no amount of busywork or cookie baking or popcorn stringing could disguise the fact that the chemistry between her and Mac Mahoney was still present and just as powerful as ever. She had to stay on her guard at all times, for to succumb to Mac's attraction was to risk Nicky, and that was something she refused to do.

"Mommy, come on!" Nicky waved at her. "We found one."

Following Mac's footprints, Marisa slogged through the snow, her eye lighting on a small, well-shaped fir at the edge of the thicket. "Oh, that's a nice one! It'll be perfect."

"Not that one," Nicky protested, his tone rife with disgust. "*This* one."

Turning, she saw Mac indicating a much larger specimen. "What do you think, Your Highness?"

She gaped. "Are you out of your mind? That thing must be ten feet tall!"

Using the butt of the ax, Mac jostled the branches to knock off the clinging snow. He hadn't shaved, and the dark shadow of his beard gave his features a piratical cast as he grinned at her. "More like twelve, I'd say."

"Out of the question!" Marisa snapped.

"But, Mommy!" Nicky wailed.

"We couldn't get it through the door. And we don't have nearly enough decorations for a tree this size. Now, this smaller one—"

The boy's mouth puckered. "Me and Mac found it. This is the one we want."

"Looks like you're outvoted, princess."

"Of all the asinine..." She ground to a halt, surveying the two faces, and knew she wasn't going to budge either of them. She threw up her hands. "Suit yourselves. But don't expect me to help you drag that monster home."

"Wouldn't dream of it," Mac answered cheerfully, hefting the ax. "This is a man thing, right, Tex? She wouldn't understand."

"Right!"

"Oh, I get it." Marisa nodded, and sarcasm laced her words. "So now we're gauging our masculinity by the size of our...tree? How typically macho of you, Mahoney. But I don't think I want Nicky picking up any of your Neanderthal ideas."

Mac shot her an annoyed glance. "Only you would turn something innocent into a feminist showdown. Just step back, will you?"

Hastily Marisa pulled Nicky back to a safe distance. The first stroke of the ax to the base of the fir sounded like a shot. The next one sent chips of bark and bare wood flying and filled the air with the pungent scent of resin. As irritated as she felt, Marisa couldn't help but admire the way Mac's shoulders heaved under his jacket, his easy strength and the way he expertly felled the tree with an economy of effort.

For a moment, it was suddenly ten years earlier, and she was enthralled with the play of bronzed muscles as she watched a younger Mac lovingly waxing his old car, cleaving the surf with powerful strokes of his arms, bending closer over her until he blotted out the sun. The memory, so long denied, now released its powerful coils, and she shuddered, the center of her melting as if it were only yesterday.

She'd been enraptured from the first by the lean strength of Mac's powerful physique, but the physical attraction had quickly led to something even more potent. His easy humor, his sharp intelligence, his drive and determination to make a name for himself in his field had won her admiration, but it was the lonely vulnerability, the uncertainty she sensed beneath his outward confidence that made her love him. For the first time in her life, someone had needed her, and she had reveled in it, and in him.

At the time, it had seemed enough.

"Timber-r-r-r!"

Nicky's jubilant cry and the fir tree crashing to the ground brought Marisa back to the present with a guilty start. Gulping, she forced the seductive images away. She couldn't afford to dwell on the past, no matter how enticing, not with Nicky's future at stake.

The boy pulled out of her grip and rushed eagerly to Mac's side. Mac plucked an abandoned bird's nest from the interior of the fallen tree and knelt to show it to the child. Their murmured conversation was incomprehensible, but they turned quick glances in Marisa's direction, then went back to their examination. Finally, Mac tucked an object into Nicky's pocket, and they stood and began to drag the tree by its base through the woods back up the slope to the lodge.

Following them, Marisa bit her lip, worried and a bit jealous of the easy camaraderie between the two. How would Nicky react when the time came to leave? She supposed she should be grateful Mac even spoke to the boy, but all the same, if Nicky became overly attached to the wandering reporter, he would only end up hurt as she had been those many years ago.

Within minutes, Nicky was red-faced and puffing from tugging at the huge tree. "Your mom looks as though she needs some help, partner," Mac said. "I can take it from here."

Hiding a grateful smile at the way Mac let the boy save face, Marisa added quickly, "I'm awfully tired, Nicky. Could you give me a hand? Look, it's starting to snow again."

Nicky's expression was dubious, but he was too breathless to protest. "We cowboys have to take care of our womenfolk, okay, Tex?" Mac prodded.

The boy gulped air, nodded, then allowed Marisa to take his hand. "Okay." The air swirled with fat, wet snowflakes as they made their way back. Marisa was thinking about hot chocolate and warm toes when Nicky gave a sudden cry. "Look, Mommy! There's another nest!" Slipping his mittened hand from hers, he dashed off the path.

Cold and cross, Marisa was in no mood to extend their outing. "Nicholas Latimore, come back here!" In the blink of an eye, the back of Nicky's bright red jacket disappeared altogether. Marisa screamed. "Nicky!"

High-stepping through the drifts, she plunged after her son. Somehow she knew that Mac had dropped the tree and was right on her heels. The slope beneath her feet changed suddenly, and she slipped and landed on her bottom, ending up right beside Nicky, who lay facedown in a snowbank. Marisa grabbed a handful of nylon ski jacket and tugged the child to his hands and knees, then frantically wiped the snow out of his nose and eyes.

Mac grabbed both of them by the collars and dragged them back to the edge of the path, all the while cursing a blue streak. "Dammit, Marisa, you scared the life out of me! What the hell's the matter with you?"

"Don't you yell at me!" Marisa gathered Nicky close. "Honey, are you all right?"

Her son wiped his wet face, looking puzzled. "I'm fine, Mommy. I just ate a mouthful of snow, that's all." He beamed and held up a black feather. "Look what I found!"

Marisa grabbed his shoulders and shook him gently. "Nicky, don't ever do that again! Don't go off the path! You could have fallen a long way and hurt yourself. Promise me!"

The boy's blue eyes were as round as pennies. "Yes, Mommy, I promise."

Mac set Nicky on his feet, then reached for Marisa's elbow. He urged her up, his voice low in her ear. "You're scaring him."

Marisa was trembling so hard she could barely stand. "There's a stream down below."

"How do you know?"

"I used to explore it...before."

"When you came here, ten years ago." His statement was flat.

"Yes." Her gaze flickered away from the accusing green intensity of his. He hadn't forgiven her for that; probably he never would. The shudder that shook her was a combination of old hurt and recent terror. "If Nicky had fallen in...."

"He didn't, so forget it. No harm done."

At Mac's brusque words, Marisa cast him a resentful look and shook off his hand. "For a man of the world, you don't know much, Mahoney. Come on, Nicky."

She grabbed her son's hand and walked him through the snow toward the lodge, leaving Mac to bring up the rear with a fervent wish that he'd slide down the mountain and right out of her life.

Unfortunately he didn't, but ended up instead on the back porch to hammer and curse a tree stand of sorts into being to support the monster fir. By the time he had maneuvered it into the two-story den, the wind had begun to howl again in earnest, but Marisa had calmed down enough to make hot chocolate for all of them. Grudgingly she had to admit that the large tree looked rather magnificent in its place of honor in the corner.

Nicky's eyes were round with awe. "This is going to be the best tree I *ever* had. Can we decorate it now? Can we?"

By unanimous vote, it was decided. So even though the radio predicted another night of howling winds, snow and sleet, and Marisa approached the project with trepidation, the evening turned into a hilarious tree-trimming party for three.

In the flickering lantern light, they strung strings of popcorn and paper chains, then roasted hot dogs for supper in the fireplace and ate the blistered frankfurters slathered with catsup and mustard. They hung the sugar cookies Marisa had baked with bits of yarn—Mac and Nicky sneaking bites for dessert—then stood back and bemoaned the bareness of the great tree.

Inspired, Marisa rummaged in the kitchen and produced some aluminum foil. She wrapped it around cardboard shapes, shiny red apples and pebbly oranges and hung them from more yarn. Mac retrieved a bale of sisal twine from the garage and uncurled it into garlands that reminded everyone of a cowboy's lasso and delighted Nicky. Following the theme, Marisa found a stack of red and blue bandannas in the napkin drawer and knotted them on the branches, then wound one of Uncle Paul's patchwork quilts around the tree's base.

As they worked, Marisa forgot the tensions that divided them, laughing at Mac's antics as he tried his hand at rope tricks for Nicky, smiling as he lifted the squealing boy to place an ornament on a high branch. It was almost as if they were a family, and as long as the weather held the outside world at bay, she was tempted to pretend.

She'd tried not to notice how Mac's hand had lingered on hers as they adjusted a stubborn loop of popcorn, nor how her breathing became erratic at his touch. When their eyes met over Nicky's head, they'd shared a silent smile together, enjoying the child's fun. But then Mac's eyes had darkened, became almost as deep as the forest, and what she'd seen there had caused her to look away in fear... and excitement. Swallowing, she resolutely pushed away such feelings as both inappropriate and too dangerous to pursue.

"It's beautiful!" Nicky gave his approval from a perch on the back of the sofa. His busy day was taking its toll, and his baby-fine lashes drooped sleepily. He twisted the corner of his favorite blanket into a tail and rubbed his eyes.

"Not bad," Mac agreed. "In fact, I'll bet it's better than anything one of your mom's fancy Hollywood designers could do. All it needs is a star at the top."

"Well, here you go." Faintly stung by Mac's remark, Marisa folded the last piece of aluminum foil over a cardboard star shape and held it out.

"You'd better put it on."

"Oh, no!" Marisa shook her head. "I'm not climbing up there!"

Mac nodded to the narrow-legged bar stool they'd used as a ladder. "That thing won't hold me up."

"Aw, Mom," Nicky protested, "go ahead. Don't be a 'fraidy cat!'"

"I'll hold you steady," Mac offered.

You let me down before. The accusation leapt into Marisa's head, and something must have shown on her face because Mac frowned. Rather than let him guess her thoughts, she moved toward the stool. "All right, but if I break my neck, I'm going to come back and haunt the both of you!"

I've been haunted by you for a decade, Mac's mind whispered. He offered his hand for support as she stepped onto the seat of the stool and was gratified to find that his fingers didn't shake, but chagrined that his heartbeat was unsteady.

"This is crazy, you know," she said, looking down into his beard-shadowed face with a nervous little laugh. "Stuck in a blizzard, taking this much trouble over a tree no one will see."

Yeah, crazy, Mac thought, supremely conscious of her small hand in his and the faint fragrance of her flowery perfume. He shook off his preoccupation, making his words matter-of-fact. "It's for the boy, isn't it? That's enough. Besides, we're almost done. And I don't know about you, but the past two days have been rather eventful. I'm ready to put my feet up for a while."

"After you shave, I hope," she sniffed. Her words were as much a defense against her own idiotic desire to run her hands over that sexy masculine stubble as a criticism of his personal habits.

He chuckled and rubbed his palm over his bristles. "Beginning to look like Man Mountain McGraw, am I? I suppose I am getting a little ripe."

No, you smell like a man. Her unbidden thought startled her. In the rarified atmosphere of Hollywood, she rarely crossed paths with a man who wasn't uptight about how he smelled, about how his hair, his teeth, his tan looked, ad nauseam. The scent of clean male musk, honest labor, and the unique essence of Mac Mahoney was far headier to her than any cologne could ever be. She swallowed hard as he continued.

"Think you could rustle me up a clean shirt? My valet forgot to pack my other bag."

Fighting a smile, she forced vinegar into her tone. "Uninvited guests can't be choosy, you know."

"Hey, what happened to old-fashioned hospitality?"

"In your case, Mahoney, it went the way of the dodo bird! Never mind, Uncle Paul probably left something in his closet you could use. I'll look just as soon as I finish here." She glanced up at the distant treetop and swallowed. "If I survive."

"Put your hand on my shoulder for balance," Mac ordered, sliding his palms up the backs of her trousered legs for support, then instantly regretting the move. *Damn, but she feels good!*

"I can't quite..." She stretched as high as she could, struggling to set the tinsel star into place. *Why does his touch have to feel so good?*

"You can do it, Mommy!" Nicky encouraged.

Rattled and reluctant, she released Mac's shoulder to use both hands and was finally able to settle the loop on the back of the star onto the topmost branch. Relief—that she could now get down and away from Mac's unsettling grip—flooded her. "There, I—whoops!"

Unbalanced, Marisa gave a tiny shriek as she toppled, knocking the stool from beneath her feet. But Mac was there, and she landed with a thud against his rocklike chest, clutching at his neck, her feet dangling well above the floor. "Relax, princess, I've got you," he rumbled.

And she realized that he did. Somehow, as he'd caught her, one hand had slipped beneath her sweater, and now his large palm lay pressed against her rib cage, a fraction below the soft swell of her breast, leaving only her thin silk chemise between his calloused hand and her satiny flesh.

Marisa's heart leapt frantically as Mac's hazel green eyes met hers. Mesmerized, she couldn't tear her gaze away. Slowly, slowly, he allowed her to slide down his body, torturing them both with the feel of her softness against his hard length. His eyes grew smoky. Marisa stifled a wild gasp as the notch of her thighs caught slightly on the fly of his jeans, and then she was past that temptation, only to find that her progress had placed her breast fully within his palm. Strong, possessive fingers closed around her flesh, and his thumb rubbed maddeningly over her silk-covered nipple. A shaft of pure sensation seared her to her very core.

Dismay made her face flame. *Oh, no, I still want him!*

Angry desire tightened his jaw. *Dammit, how can I still want her?*

"Mommy, are you okay? Your face is all red."

Gulping, Marisa hastily disentangled herself and backed up against the sofa, where Nicky was watching with avid eyes. "I—I'm fine, kiddo."

"You got a fever?" Nicky laid the back of his small hand against her forehead in a sympathetic gesture she'd used a million times on him. His young voice held a solemn conviction. "You need to go to bed."

Mac snorted. "You don't know the half of it, buddy."

Marisa's face flamed again, this time in outrage. She glanced at her bewildered son and forced a smile. "Crawl under those covers, cowpoke. It's way past your bedtime."

Nicky obediently tucked his feet under the blankets and snuggled down, already drowsy. "You coming to sleep now, too, Mommy?"

"Not just yet. I—I've got to find a clean shirt for Mac first." *And a noose.*

Placing a kiss on her son's forehead, Marisa shot her unwelcome guest a look that was pure venom, then picked up one of the lanterns and stormed up the staircase, every fiber of her body quivering with anger and something she couldn't—or wouldn't—identify.

In the chilly upstairs bedroom, she rummaged through Paul's closet muttering imprecations, pulling sweatpants and flannel shirts off their hangers and flinging them to the floor with unrestrained violence. She hesitated only once, at an old fringed suede vest, a holdover from the sixties that she instantly knew would make a fine pair of cowboy chaps to accompany Nicky's stick horse. After setting the vest aside, she grabbed up the pile of clothing, then gave a slight gasp of surprise as Mac strode boldly into the room.

Pushing the door shut behind him with an ominous click, he drawled, "I'm damned sick of you running out on me, princess."

"Tough luck, Mahoney. Here." She tossed the clothes at him. "Try to make yourself presentable—if that's possible. I'm going to bed."

The clothes fluttered to the floor. He made no move to pick them up, but caught her arm as she tried to move past him. "I want to talk."

She lifted her chin. "Why? We have nothing to say to each other."

"That's where you're wrong. After all, we seemed to be doing pretty well until just a moment ago."

"And leave it to you to ruin everything," she said bitterly.

Mac's expression became mocking. "Oh, that's right, look for a whipping boy. We're back to that prima donna crap you love so much." He pulled her closer, bending his head so that they were nearly nose-to-nose. "Tell me you didn't see this coming."

She breathed defiance. "All I see is that you haven't changed at all!"

"Nor have you. Which should make it that much easier."

She frowned, her blue eyes wide and wary. "Make what easier?"

"The reckoning you owe me." In the flickering lantern light, his features could have been cast in stone. "You ran out on me ten years ago without a word. The way I figure, it's past time for some answers, and tonight I'm getting them—one way or another."

Four

―――

"**I** don't owe you anything, Mahoney!"

"And just how do you figure that?" Mac's hand tightened around her arm. "We were living together! What was I supposed to think when I came home to find you'd moved out, lock, stock and barrel? No warning, no note of explanation—not to mention *apology*. Didn't that fancy finishing school of yours teach you anything about etiquette, for Pete's sake?"

Marisa lifted her chin to glare at him. "Sorry, I never took How to End a Love Affair 101."

"Dammit, Marisa! You left me with my guts bleeding!" His eyes had lost their usual emerald gleam, leaving only the bleakest brown. "At least tell me why."

"Why? *Why?*" Her voice dripped disdain. "Boy, was I right! You never took the trouble to know me at all, did you?"

"Inside and out, baby. Every sweet inch of you—that's how well I knew you."

She wrenched her arm free, her eyes blazing. "Wrong. You want to know why I had to leave, why you *forced* me to go? All right, I'll tell you, much good it'll do! You wouldn't listen then, and I doubt if you can bear to hear it now."

"What the hell are you babbling about?"

"You, Mahoney! Yes, I left you. I ran, I admit it. *But you drove me to it.*"

He threw up his hands. "Jeez, I might have known you'd try to blame it on me. Typical irrational female excuse!"

"You're doing it again, refusing to understand what I'm trying to tell you. But that's exactly my point, Mahoney." Her shoulders slumped. "You said you loved me, then dismissed everything that was important to me."

"Like what, for instance?"

"Like putting down roots. Like pursuing my craft."

"As a *soap opera* actress, I suppose? I wanted better for you than that!" Mac jammed fingers through his dark hair in a gesture of pure disgust. "For heaven's sake, woman! You were the most promising journalist on the whole damn West Coast. And you gave it all up—for what?"

"For a chance to create something for myself."

Mac's craggy features registered disbelief. "Don't you understand you were talented enough to have made a difference? You could have been part of my team. We could have accomplished something important together, something lasting."

"That was your dream, Mac," she said softly. "Not mine."

"But—"

Tiredly she shoved golden tendrils that had fallen from her ponytail out of her face and lifted a hand to interrupt. "No, you started this. Hear me out."

The muscle in the side of his beard-shadowed jaw knotted, but he crossed his arms over his chest and nodded curtly. "All right. I'm listening."

Marisa swallowed, trying to force back a lump swelling in her throat. She would not cry. She wouldn't. Needing some distance, she moved around the foot of Paul's antique oak bedstead and leaned her shoulder against the window frame, shivering as she stared out at the blizzard-tossed blackness.

His derisive words speared her across the dimly lit room. "Don't you know where to start? How about the day you married Victor Latimore?"

Her head snapped around. "Victor has nothing to do with this. With us. He never did."

"Nice to know."

"The problem with you is that you just can't keep your mouth shut, Mahoney." Fists clenched, she turned to face him. "You were always so busy trying to save the world, you never could see that I might need to create something valuable of my own."

"Excuse me, I guess I missed the press release announcing that your Dinah Dillman character had become the new Mother Theresa. What next—sainthood?"

"That's right, crack jokes. You're so good at making people feel small. You're an expert at grinding your subject under your heel until he squeals for mercy!"

Mac shrugged. "Never said the pursuit of truth wasn't painful, honey."

"Believe me, I'm fully aware that you never blink an eye at the prospect of hurting someone with the 'truth,'" she said, her voice bitter. "Only look at what it's doing to Nicky and me! And how did you think it made me feel when you were so openly contemptuous of my acting? I'm good at what I do! Entertaining people gives me a great deal of creative and personal satisfaction."

"But look at what you threw away—"

"I didn't throw anything away! I made a *choice*."

"Right. You chose not to be with me."

She paled, and her lips barely moved. "You make it sound so easy. It was the hardest decision I've ever had to make."

"How hard could it be?" He laughed, a harsh sound that held no humor. "Pack a bikini, leave a key, then hippity-hop home to your mom and dad."

"You know that isn't true. My parents were the last people I wanted to see. Why should I? They never needed or supported me. Why waste time on their only offspring when there are so many more enjoyable pastimes—yachting the seven seas, brawling like stevedores in every port, drinking themselves to early deaths. So I came here." Her voice shook with a sudden quaver. "It took a long time for me to get over you."

Unmoved, Mac stared at her, his expression mocking. "Oh, and that's supposed to make me feel bad?"

"You want an apology? You can have it. I'm sorry, Mac. It was wrong of me to leave in such a hurried fashion. My only excuse is that I was young and inexperienced and hurting. At the time there didn't seem any other way."

He snorted. "Another convenient rationalization."

Marisa lifted her hands in appeal. "You made it clear where you were going, that there wasn't room for compromise or concessions. The vagabond life you relished—I grew up with that, and I hated it! Never knowing who I was, or where I belonged." Her eyes, turbulent indigo, begged for understanding. "I couldn't settle for that, not for myself or the children I wanted! I tried to tell you that, over and over. Don't you remember?"

He waved a dismissive hand. "I suppose. Vaguely."

Anger flared white-hot within her. "I thought as much. These were things I felt so strongly about, and you can't even remember!"

"I remember how good it was with us, how I could make you go up in flames. We used to burn up the sheets."

"You egotistical—" She spluttered, furious. "The tears I shed over you were a waste of good saltwater."

He smiled, a feral baring of teeth. "But great practice for your career as Queen of the Soaps, right, princess?"

Fury stained her cheeks crimson, and she answered with a taunt of her own. "Your real problem, Mahoney, is that you just can't take that I outgrew my awe of the hotshot reporter—leather jacket, dark sunglasses, world-weary expression and all. Admit it, you couldn't handle my wanting to be a part of the decision making about our life together, instead of just your favorite adoring groupie!"

"It wasn't like that."

"Oh, no? You may as well 'fess up, Mahoney. I know what this is really about. When I left, only your pride was hurt."

Under his stubble, his skin flushed a dull scarlet. "You don't have any idea what I felt."

Her laugh was pained. "Heck, you were probably relieved! As soon as I quit worshiping at your feet and wanted to become a real partner, it quickly became clear that you weren't really in love with me at all—only this image you had of me."

Mac rounded the foot of the bed and came toward her, breathing hard. "How can you say that?" he challenged. "I loved you."

She shook her head sadly. "Maybe you loved what you thought you could make me, but all you saw when you looked at me was a reflection of yourself. You never really knew me at all, Mac."

"Did you learn all this psychological mumbo jumbo on 'Time Won't Tell'? It's really quite convincing—for a bunch of bull."

"You're so strong, Mac, but you have no idea how over-powering that can be. You were swallowing me alive." She blinked, fighting back the moisture stinging behind her lids. "I tried to tell you what I was feeling, but you just laughed it off or took me to bed until I forgot. What kind of a relationship was that?"

"It worked for me."

His flippancy stabbed her like a knife. "You still don't understand, do you? My small dreams were just as valid as your larger ones, but we couldn't communicate, so there was no middle ground. All or nothing—your way. I was so desperate, in the end all I could do was run or end up losing everything—even my own identity."

For a moment, Mac stood silently. Then he lifted his hands and clapped them together once, twice. "Quite a performance."

He might as well have slapped her. For a stunned instant, she couldn't move, then a cry of pure anguish escaped her lips. Blindly, knowing only that she had to escape, she tried to push past him.

"Oh, no, you don't." Mac swung her around and pressed her against the wall. Looming over her, he easily controlled her struggles. "You're not running out on me again, not before I get to the truth."

With a dry sob of despair, she pushed at his flannel-covered chest. "You wouldn't recognize the truth if it came up and bit you!"

"You're wrong, princess. I've been in the truth business so long I can smell a lie a mile away. Why don't you just give it to me straight—you stopped loving me and took the easy way out. Be honest about that, at least."

"Coming clean with you doesn't work," she choked. "You don't believe your own ears. Let me go."

He shook her. "Tell me. I can take that you stopped caring. Was there another man already? Latimore?"

Shocked, she shook her head. "No! I didn't even meet Victor until two years later."

"So what was it? The workingman's grime under my nails? My lack of the proper social connections? Surely you remember the one thing that made you turn your back on the best thing you'd ever had."

"What I don't remember is your being intentionally cruel," she said, her voice trembling.

"And I guess I was so blind that I didn't see what a spoiled, selfish creature you were."

"That's not true—"

"Don't bother to deny it. Facing the lover you were abandoning might have tarnished your self-image, and Miss All-American Girl couldn't stand that. Admit it!"

Frantic to be free of him, of the hurt she'd pretended was long dead and buried but was now making fresh wounds in her heart, she answered recklessly. "Yes! It's true. Anything—"

"What a coward you are." Tangling his fingers in her hair, he jerked her face to his, his expression grim and vengeful. "Couldn't face me then. Can't face *this* now." Before she could register his intent, his mouth covered hers. His lips were hard and plundering, hurtful and... utterly needy.

Stunned by the realization that she'd hurt this man more deeply than she'd ever dreamed, Marisa stopped fighting him, allowing him to take his revenge where he would. It was little enough to expiate her guilt, especially when his mouth softened, became beguiling, and the erotic rasp of his stubbled skin on hers defined their essential differences, recalling to her with a poignancy that brought tears all that she had missed in the years since she had last known this man's touch.

Mac drew back, breathing hard, confusion riding his countenance like a storm cloud. She'd thought the sight of her tears might give him some satisfaction, but she saw only regret. Whether it was a trick of the fitful lantern light or her own self-delusion, she reacted instinctively, tightening her fingers without thought in the soft flannel of his shirt and dragging his head down to hers.

Resisting, suspicious, he flinched backward. She would have none of it and pressed against him, murmuring over his lips. "Kiss me back, Mahoney. And you called *me* a coward..."

With a growl, he slanted his mouth over hers, releasing her head to pull her into a bone-crushing embrace. Marisa reveled in his strength, the power that simmered just beneath his skin. If she could only melt into that steely warmth....

Flicking the tip of her tongue over his bottom lip, she enticed and invited, then was rewarded when he thrust his tongue into her mouth, boldly invading. Staking a claim that could not be denied, he explored every inch of the sweet cavern. Marisa's knees lost the ability to support her, and she slid her arms around his neck to keep from falling.

Mac was none too steady himself. Bracing one palm against the wall at her back, he pressed his lower body against her belly, evoking a low vibration of sound from Marisa of pure carnality. Tongues darted, mating, licking. Mouths melded, seeking, taking.

Marisa buried her fingers in the silky darkness of Mac's hair, stroking his nape, straining to get even closer. Spangles danced behind her eyes, and she couldn't see, couldn't breathe, could only feel. It was an oblivion she welcomed.

After an eternity of sensation, her tortured lungs demanded air. Sensing her need, Mac released her lips, transferring his mouth to the tender curve of her neck and sending rivers of excitement rushing to every extremity.

Gasping, Marisa threw back her head and arched against him, allowing him greater access. Untangling her fingers from his hair, she slid them beneath his collar to explore the burnished muscles of his powerful neck. She felt him shudder as her fingertips traced the tendons there. Emboldened, she outlined his collarbone, then counted the erratic pulse beating at the base of his throat. Her own blood was rushing so fast she could hear nothing but the roar of wildfire flooding her veins.

Mac's lips were everywhere, producing delicious shivers on her neck, tantalizing the velvety underside of her earlobe, grazing along the delicate bones in her cheek and jaw, kissing away the remnants of moisture at the corners of her eyes. When he found her mouth again, a moan rumbled deep in his chest, almost as if he was in pain, and he slipped both hands beneath the hem of her sweater and rode them up her rib cage until the lush swell of her breasts filled his palms.

They both moaned then.

Impatient, he circled the crests with his thumbs, and mimicked the motion inside her mouth with his tongue. Marisa's core became molten with desire. Lifting his head, he pulled her sweater up and over and flung it across the chilly room, leaving her standing in slacks and silky, lace-edged chemise. Whether from the coolness of the air or his heated regard, her nipples pebbled into hard buds, poking impudently against the rose-colored silk, and his eyes blazed emerald.

His index finger hooked under one slender spaghetti strap, he tugged it slowly down her shoulder and sucked in a harsh breath as the garment caught on the nubby tip of her nipple. Marisa felt it catch, and strangely the tingling sensation seemed to lodge between her legs.

Mac cupped her bottom and pulled her into the cradle of his thighs, and she gasped again, feeling the rock-hard contour of his arousal pressed intimately to her. He tugged the chemise strap harder, and it slid free, revealing the creamy, rose and white lushness of her to his gaze.

As though he had no choice, Mac bent slightly to run the tip of his tongue down her breastbone. The wet coolness made her shiver uncontrollably, but when he took the rosy nipple between his lips and suckled, it was fire that consumed Marisa.

Crying out, she clutched at his shoulders, trying to reach him, sprinkling kisses on the top of his head, the curl of his ear, anywhere she could touch. His mouth was ardent on her flesh, the arousing rasp of his tongue undisciplined, and she was falling, falling. . . .

Mac caught her in his arms and carried her to the quilt-covered bed, then pressed her down against the soft patchwork. He took her mouth again in a drugging kiss, pushing the chemise completely off her shoulders so that it puddled at her waistline. His knee moved aggressively, parting her legs. Frantic to touch him, Marisa tugged his shirttail free of his jeans, then shoved her hands beneath his undershirt to press her palms against his hair-dusted chest. When her nails scraped his flat nipples, he jerked uncontrollably.

Evoking such a powerful a reaction from him filled her with satisfaction, but it was hard to smile with his mouth consuming hers. Still, he seemed to sense her triumph, and a low, mating sound rumbled in his throat. Sliding an arm beneath her back, he lifted her to him, then worshiped the lushness of her breasts with his open mouth. She arched, lasped his head between her hands, holding him at the most ensitive spots, quivering with the sweet rush of passion.

Expertly he flicked the button at her waistband, opened he zipper and slid his fingers down her flat stomach and nder the elastic of her bikini panties, sifting through the rinkling hair at the top of her thighs.

The reality of where this was leading slammed into Ma-isa's consciousness, and she caught his wrist. Her nearly verwhelming need to feel his intimate touch warred with er absolute fear of the consequences—for her, for Nicky— t such a capitulation. The dilemma made her moan. "No, Mac, no, this isn't good."

"It isn't?" He breathed against her breast, amused. "Could have fooled me."

"No, I mean—" She groaned again. "It's good—you lon't know—but it's still a bad idea."

"The chemistry's still there. Don't deny it." Raising his nead, he met her gaze, then boldly, brazenly, cupped her mound. "We've always had this." She was so near the flash voint she couldn't catch her breath. "You used to like it."

"Unfortunately it appears I still do." Blushing furiously, ner tone rueful, she drew his hand away.

His dark brows lowered in a startled frown. "So what are ve going to do about it?"

"Nothing." She shook her head, and the tumbled gold of ner hair shimmered on her creamy shoulders. "It wasn't nough then. It isn't now."

Gazing avidly at her nudity, he swallowed, and his eyes larkened. "It could be."

"For how long? A night? A day?" Her voice was a pain-ul whisper. How could she resume a relationship with a nan who held himself under such tight control he couldn't ven admit to needing an emotional life of his own? "Too isky for my tastes, Mac. I'm not into masochism."

He was silent a long moment, then pushed himself to his feet, his gaze dragging away from her with an effort. "Yeah. Neither am I."

Deprived of his presence, she shivered suddenly, chilled in the cold room. She sat up, quickly adjusted her clothing and looked around for her sweater. She found it in a wad on the floor and slipped it on, still shaking with cold and the afterquakes of unfulfilled arousal.

Mac was having his own problems. His back turned, he braced his hands on either side of the window frame and rested his forehead against the frosted glass, breathing in gusty gulps as he sought to regain control. "Sorry," he mumbled. "My mistake."

Not entirely, she admitted to herself. She patted and tucked at the bed, nervously removing all evidence of their encounter as though that could erase it from their minds. "Never mind. The snow makes people crazy," she said, shrugging.

"It wasn't the snow." He turned, and his expression changed. "I didn't mean to hurt you."

"What?" She raised her fingers to trace her swollen lips, the abrasions his beard had left on her tender skin. Knowing he'd marked her with his passion made her feel shaky inside. "It's no matter."

"Yeah, well, I'd better get cleaned up, anyway." He started for the door, pausing only to scoop up the clothing she'd tossed at him a lifetime earlier. Tugging the hem of her sweater, Marisa followed him, feeling hesitant and adrift, as though she were a ship lost in uncharted waters. It was disconcerting to move from the height of passion to common banalities so rapidly. But if he could do it, so could she!

"I—I'll heat some wash water for you."

He paused in the doorway, and the look he sent her was wry. "Don't bother. Cold shower, Marisa. Your fault. Get it?"

Marisa couldn't help it. She laughed.

"It's good to hear you do that," he said.

"I'm still known to do so on occasion."

"Lot to think about." The small nod of his head indicated both their argument and the fireworks that followed.

She licked her lips, then nearly groaned to find his flavor still lingering there. "Yes."

"Decided what you're going to do about Nicky?"

The unexpected question made her remember why Mac Mahoney was here. Not for revenge. Not for an old love. *For the story.* How could she have forgotten? She tilted her chin. "Love him. Raise him. Protect him."

"You're not the only one involved in his life anymore."

"I'm the only one who counts."

"You're going to have to deal with—"

"Don't you tell me how to live my life or how to protect my child! I've done nothing wrong, and neither has Nicky." Despite the sweater, she felt chilled again, this time to the bone. "Why should the innocent be punished?"

"No one wants to punish you, Marisa."

She arched one eyebrow. "No?"

Mac let out a deep breath. "No. What purpose would it serve?"

"You tell me."

"It's the truth that counts. And I'll have it, one way or another. Permanently shutting down Dr. Morris's baby mill has to take precedence over personal considerations."

"Back off, Mac," she warned, her expression fierce. "No matter what you think, this is not your business. I won't tolerate your hounding us. You're here on sufferance, remember?"

"I've got a job to do."

"At our expense?" She snatched the discarded suede vest from the foot of the bed, and her voice was scathing. "That hardly makes you the guy in the white hat, now does it?"

"I'm not the villain in this piece, either," he protested.

She stepped past him, and her eyes were dark with pain. "That, Mr. Mahoney, is entirely a matter of opinion."

A chunk of frozen slush rolled off Mac's armload of wood and landed in his boot to trickle icy moisture down his fresh socks. Deciding he'd already brought in enough wood to see them through the night, he dropped his burden back into the pile on the rear veranda of the lodge and stepped into the lee of the wall out of the wind, automatically patting his parka pockets.

He felt the familiar outlines of notebook and pens, keys, wallet and various electronic devices no self-respecting journalist would be without these days—but no cigarettes. Then he realized what he was doing and mouthed an expletive. He'd given up smoking three years ago—it was rather amazing what kind of vows a man would make and keep when he was pinned down by an IRA sniper—and reaching for a smoke only proved what a state Marisa had gotten him into!

Mac tucked his hands under his armpits and stared, grim-faced, out into the darkness. The wind was still a howling banshee, but the snow seemed to have let up a bit. And Mac knew he was all kinds of stupid to venture out into the frigid air right after a shave, a spot bath and a change of clothes. Come morning, he'd be chapped in places he didn't even know he had.

Still, with Marisa pointedly ignoring him as she crept around the lodge, cutting and stitching whatever it was she was putting together for Nicky's Christmas, he'd needed a

moment of solitude—even if it was in subfreezing weather—
to regain his equilibrium.

Damn stubborn woman! Despite everything, it was abun-
dantly clear that they'd lost none of their compatibility in
bed. They could have been cosily basking in the afterglow
at this very moment but for her scruples. Instead, she was
sulking, and he was freezing. Too bad the young woman
who'd been sweetness itself had become a sharp-tongued
thirty-year-old termagant.

Mac supposed he ought to be grateful. The last thing he
needed was an entanglement right now—especially in the
middle of his big story! Still, the way Marisa had re-
sponded—hell, the way *he'd* nearly gone off like a Fourth
of July firecracker—gave a man plenty to fantasize about.

And as for all that rigmarole about his being the reason
she'd left him, that was just a woman's rationalization,
wasn't it? Eating her alive, indeed! He'd communicated.
Hell, that was his business! Just because he'd wanted more
for her than a miserable actress's life...but she'd risen to the
top of her profession, an inner voice reminded him. Was it
the fact that she'd done it without him that rankled so
badly? Had he really been so blinded by his own ambitions
and a save-the-world attitude that he hadn't been able to see,
much less support, what she really needed?

Grunting, Mac forcibly pushed the uncomfortable questions from his mind and turned his thoughts to what his
producer, Tom Powell, was doing at that moment. Not
preparing to spend a holiday with his family, Mac was certain. No, after running off a succession of wives, Tom was
alone, too, and more driven than Mac ever wanted to be.
Hell, Tom was probably in the editing studio recutting the
Dr. Franco Morris background material for the hundredth
time, waiting with baited breath for Mac to show up with the
rest of the juicy story and smacking his lips at the thought

of a Hollywood soap star, a sleazy adoption deal and a sensational scandal all rolled into one neat package.

Mac's mouth twisted. Yeah, he and Tom made a good team, and this deal with INN would certainly take the pressure off financially. He just hadn't counted on it being so damn difficult to separate the personal from the professional this go-round.

Shivering, Mac stomped the snow from his boots and went inside. Nicky was sound asleep in his spot on the old sofa, but Marisa was nowhere to be seen. Mac took off his boots by the back door. Through the slats of the den balcony he could see a soft glow emanating from an upstairs room, indicating she was still at work on her projects. With the next day Christmas Eve, there was no time to dally.

Mac himself had managed to slip away a few minutes earlier that morning to patch up the old sled, sand it down with steel wool, then give it a coat of red spray paint. The results were impressive, even if he did say so himself. Now if it would only warm up enough for the paint to dry properly, everything be in fine shape. The thought of Nicky's pleasure when he saw the sled Christmas morning made Mac's mouth tilt in a small smile. Almost as good as a Tonka dragline.

With the pungent scent of freshly cut evergreen tickling his nose, Mac shucked off his jacket, tossed it on a chair, then, with an affectionate glance at Nicky's fair head, thought better of it and hung it on the rack beside the front door. No use leaving temptation in the inquisitive little rascal's way. They'd be busy enough tomorrow putting the finishing touches on his mother's earrings to keep him out of trouble. Maybe.

Clad in one of Paul's worn flannel shirts and a pair of sagging gray sweatpants, Mac punched up the fire and put on extra wood for the night. After that, there didn't seem to be any reason to put off the inevitable. With one last speculative look upstairs, he shrugged and lay down on his mattress.

Mac was just drifting off when Nicky's sharp cry of terror startled him bolt upright. For a confused moment, he was back on assignment in Beirut, and the shelling had started again, raining death and destruction to the cries of women and children. The sight of Nicky burrowing in the covers in a frenzy of night-driven fear banished the vision. Rolling to his knees beside the sofa, he reached instinctively for the sobbing child.

"What is it, little partner? Hey, it's all right."

"Dog," Nicky choked, his plump arms latching onto Mac's neck in a grip of pure desperation. Mac could feel the rapid scamper of Nicky's heart through the wall of his own chest. "Bad dog. With teeth . . ."

Mac stroked the child's head. "It's just a dream."

"Don't let him get me!"

"No, I won't. We'll run the yellow-bellied varmint right out of town. Don't you worry, Deputy. Sheriff Mac has everything under control."

"Promise?" The word was a suspicious snuffle.

"On my honor as a cowboy." Automatically, Mac kissed the top of the boy's head and gave him a squeeze.

When he looked up, he saw Marisa frozen at the base of the stairs, clutching a newspaper-wrapped bundle to her chest. Her expression held concern and a peculiar element of poignant longing.

It came to Mac in that instant that this beautiful madonna was not the same woman he'd once known. No, she was stronger, surer of herself and her place in the universe. Maturity and motherhood had tempered her like fine steel, had given her the depth and purpose that had been missing in the younger Marisa he'd once loved.

And if he'd been smarter and luckier, she might have been his, the child he comforted his own. He might have seen her grow from green girl to confident, intriguing woman and been a part of the process that transformed her. He knew then what he'd lost, and the anger he'd nurtured for so long dissolved, leaving behind only an unutterable sense of grief.

"I'm okay," Nicky muttered, rubbing chubby knuckles over his damp cheeks. "I know cowboys ain't supposed to cry."

Mac swallowed hard. "Sometimes they do, partner. Sometimes they do."

Five

It was a picture-perfect Christmas Eve.

Marisa stumbled to the kitchen early the next morning and came up short in wonder at the pristine scene displayed beyond the window. Brilliant sunshine sparkled on diamond-tipped snowdrifts, the atmosphere was crystal clear all the way to the distant mountain peaks, and the sky was so blue it hurt the eyes. It was a glorious day—straight off of a greeting card—but it was the blessed hush that was so enthralling, for the air was still and everything in the world was at peace at last.

At least on the outside.

Marisa found it ironic that the fitful weather had dissipated just as the emotional storm within her had become ever more turbulent.

Reaching for the coffeepot, she tried not to think of the scene she'd witnessed the evening before, but nothing could erase the impact that finding Mac comforting her son with such tenderness had made. Nicky had slipped easily back to dreamland following his nightmare, but Marisa had wrestled with her own preconceived notions about Mac Mahoney well into the night.

Had she misjudged Mac? Was there a softness somewhere underneath all that hard, no-nonsense strength that she'd overlooked? After the wanton way she'd behaved in his arms, she was hardly in a position to be objective! While a purely physical relationship wasn't enough for her long-term, there was something so compelling about Mac, something that touched her deepest soul even now. If only they weren't in opposition over his Dr. Morris exposé, then things might be very different between them. She shivered, realizing such thoughts were seductive, dangerous and yet ... and yet ...

"You going to marry that thing or make coffee in it?" Mac leaned against the doorway, glowering at her, haggard as an old bear in Paul's disreputable shirt and a pair of worn sweatpants, which sagged dangerously low on his lean hips. Sleepy-eyed, his whiskey-dark hair falling onto his forehead, a glimpse of navel winking from beneath his waistband, he looked so incredibly masculine, so blatantly sexy, that Marisa turned away in haste, reaching blindly for the bottled water.

"What's got your bustle in an uproar this morning, Mahoney?" She fought to keep her voice even. "Oh, I forgot. A foul mood is your normal modus operandi, isn't it?"

Surprisingly he gave a snort of laughter. "You know, I've decided I like this change in you, princess. You give as good as you get these days."

Marisa set the coffeepot on the stove and shoved her disheveled hair out of her face. She gave a tired sigh. "Let's not fight, Mac. It's Christmas Eve, the sun is shining, and you promised we'd have a cease-fire for Nicky's sake."

Frowning, he stepped to her side, sliding his hand under her hair and began to gently massage her tensed shoulders beneath the purple sweat suit she'd slept in. "I meant it as a compliment, honey."

"Oh." The pressure of his fingers felt so good she arched her neck like a cat. "With you it's hard to tell sometimes."

"I know. I'm really inscrutable, aren't I?" His lips twitched. "Especially before I've had my caffeine."

"Idiot." She shook her head, but the word held no rancor.

Releasing her, he widened his eyes and gave her his best indignant Tommy Smothers impression. "Oh *yeah?* Well, I know something you don't know!"

"What? Mother liked you best?"

The humor in his hazel green eyes faded. Solemnly, he ran his knuckle down her cheek. "Considering both our choices of mothers, I plead the Fifth on that one. No, what I meant was *this.*" Reaching behind her, he flicked a wall switch. The overhead fluorescent light buzzed, then flooded the kitchen with light.

"Power!" Marisa cried, delighted. "When did this happen?"

"Sometime during the night, I suppose."

"Heat, running water, a real bath!" she enthused, dancing a little jig. "I'll go turn on the furnace. Do you think you can find the main water valve? How long does it take a water heater to warm up? I—"

Despite himself, he grinned. "So much for your pioneer spirit, huh, Marisa?"

Miffed, she protested. "I did all right, didn't I? Just because I prefer modern conveniences—"

"Yeah." Touching her face again, he broke off her tirade, his expression both indulgent and admiring. "Yeah, you did all right."

His caress was so unsettling, she moved away in haste and practically snatched up the wall phone's receiver on the pretext of checking it. Only after she heard nothing on the line and felt a surge of relief did she realize she'd dreaded what she might find. Her voice was composed when she spoke. "The phone lines are still down, though."

"Whether you like it or not, you can't hide out from the world forever, Marisa."

"I'm not hiding out," she retorted tartly. "I'm on a holiday hiatus. What about the roads?"

"Unless things really start to thaw, my guess is it'll still be a day or two before they'll be clear enough to use, especially up here."

"So we're still stuck."

"For the time being."

"I suppose it's best to be calm and philosophical about these things."

"Oh, yes, indeed. I can see you're remarkably calm."

His mocking tone made her blush. Suddenly she found this game of cat and mouse they were playing together tiresome. Yet, there didn't appear any way out. Impasse.

"Mommy! Mommy, come see!" Like a tornado, Nicky barreled into the kitchen. He grabbed hold of Marisa's hand and dragged her toward the den. "You gotta see. The 'toons are on!"

Gratefully Marisa allowed her pajama-clad child to pull her into the other room to inspect the television on the bookcase. Nicky was more concerned by the absence of his favorite cable programs than he was with the intricacies of how the electricity had been restored. Explaining that Uncle Paul's antenna couldn't pick up all the usual stations, and that the programming was no doubt different due to the holidays, anyway, Marisa helped the boy check out the various channels.

After a few minutes, Mac sauntered in carrying two steaming mugs of coffee and handed one to Marisa, fixed just as she liked. "Thanks," she murmured, and took a sip. Why was everything this man did a continual surprise?

"No problem. Hey, hold up there a minute, partner."

Nicky paused with his finger over the channel changer button. The face of a familiar morning personality flashed on the screen. Nicky's tone was disgusted. "Oh, that's just news."

"I'll turn it back over to you in a sec, okay?" Mac asked. "Just want to catch the headlines."

Nicky rolled his eyes at adult eccentricities but dutifully folded his arms and waited. Over the rim of her cup, Marisa watched Mac's face as he listened to the reports of national political machinations, global civil unrest and the usual holiday human interest features. His expression was intent, intelligent and a tad impatient.

This was his world, Marisa knew, and it was obvious he was missing it, champing at the bit to get back into the loop. And there was no doubt Mac Mahoney was one of the best, but seeing him this way only underscored the differences in outlook that had separated them before. He was ready to go gallivanting off on the next assignment no matter how difficult or dangerous, or who was left waiting at home. The essential fact that they wanted different things from life had never changed, and she'd better not forget it.

"Look, Mommy! There's Aunt Carlene!"

Marisa snapped her gaze from Mac's countenance to the picture on the screen. A TV reporter shoved a microphone into her agent's face. While Carlene Mendez's lips moved, a voice-over announced:

"And now in entertainment news, a spokesperson for actress Marisa Rourke said in a recent statement that the star of top-rated soap 'Time Won't Tell' is on holiday with family and can't be reached for comment on the Dr. Franco—''

"Change the channel, Nicky," she ordered hoarsely.

"Okay, Mac?"

"Go ahead, partner."

Gleefully Nicky complied, settling cross-legged before a repeat of Dr. Seuss's *How the Grinch Stole Christmas* animated feature.

"I told you the world wouldn't go away," Mac said quietly. "When are you going to let others stop doing the talking for you and take the opportunity I'm offering?"

Pressing fingertips to a sudden pain in her temple, Marisa turned away and scanned the piles of blankets and makeshift beds and the majestic Christmas tree with its homey assortment of ornaments as if she'd never seen them before. Everything she'd been trying to ignore since she reached the lodge tumbled pell-mell in her brain.

She felt gratitude that Carlene appeared to be coping despite Marisa's vanishing without a trace. She worried about the crew of "Time Won't Tell." She'd left her friends there in the lurch. The producers and writers could only cover her absence for a limited time, then her job would be in jeopardy, contract or not. But most troubling of all was the terror that someone—for whatever reasons, right or wrong—would take her most precious possession . . . her son.

Mac was right, Marisa thought miserably, folding her trembling hands around her mug. She really was a coward when it came to confrontation. She preferred harmony, trying to work her way around the outside edges of a disagreeable situation rather than facing it head-on. It was how she'd survived her parents' stormy marriage, and lessons taught so early were hard to unlearn. Her breakup with Mac, her guilt and failures with Victor, and now the question of Nicky's legal parentage and his future—how she wished she'd never had to face any of them! But she couldn't play the ostrich this time.

Mac had been nearer to the truth than he'd known when he'd accused her of trying to leave the country. She had friends in Montreal, an acquaintance with a villa in Monaco. There were ways to drop off the face of the earth for a while, even with a face that was almost as famous in Europe as it was in the U.S., thanks to overseas syndication. To protect her child, she'd give up everything, go anywhere, do anything!

But what's best for Nicky? Uprooting him, taking him away from all that was familiar—or taking the chance that the courts might turn him over to his birth mother out of some misguided sense of "justice"? Even a battery of the best-paid lawyers couldn't guarantee the outcome of such a convoluted moral dilemma. Losing her son would destroy her, Marisa knew. And, although children were resilient, being torn from the only mother he'd ever known couldn't help but be traumatic for a child old enough to remember, to hurt, to grieve.

Moving to the tree, Marisa lovingly touched one of the multicolored paper chains she and Nicky had made. She would have to make a decision eventually, but as long as they remained stranded here, she had a reprieve. Perhaps, if she had enough time, she could make the right choices for both Nicky and everyone involved. Time was what she needed, but now that the storm was over, it was running out. Mac had found her with ease, and other equally determined reporters on the trail of a sensational story might follow at any moment. She couldn't dodge the spotlight forever.

"Marisa? Are you all right?" She looked up to find Mac beside her, his craggy features etched with concern. Mac had started all this, but it was difficult to remember her anger with him when he looked at her with such sympathy in his eyes.

A sudden thought struck her. What if she made him an ally instead of her enemy? He had warm feelings for Nicky already. If she could make Mac see what Nicky meant to her, perhaps she could convince him to postpone the pursuit of his story long enough to let her make the right decision. Mac was a reasonable man. But she'd been so hostile, she hadn't even given him a chance to see things from her perspective. She had to try. It was her only option.

He was still watching her, waiting for her response. She forced a smile. "I'm okay. And as far as what you're offering... let me think about it?"

Surprised, skeptical, but somewhat gratified, he nodded. "Sure."

"I just thought of another reason why I'm glad the power's back on." Behind them, Nicky shrieked with laughter as the Grinch transformed his dog into a reluctant reindeer.

Mac grinned. "You mean besides hot baths and a chance to indulge in a little mindless entertainment?"

Laughing, she nodded. "Yes, I do. You hungry?"

"Uh, yeah. Always."

"Then let's go plug in Uncle Paul's waffle iron and see what happens."

Piles of waffles and gallons of maple syrup later, Marisa watched the two men of the house huddle over a secret project at the kitchen table. From Nicky's excited looks and hastily hidden activities whenever she came near, Marisa had no doubts that whatever they were working on was meant for her.

Seeing Mac take the time to help and humor a little boy warmed Marisa's heart as much as the now-functioning furnace warmed the lodge. As she cleaned the kitchen, she pretended not to notice their whispered consultation, Nicky's adamant rejection of Mac's suggestion, then Mac's cajoling him into an apparent concession. It was an interesting exchange, and she thoroughly enjoyed her covert observations as she tended to a few domestic chores.

Mac had returned his mattress to its rightful place, which allowed her to tidy the den for the first time since their arrival. The kink in the small of her back was a constant reminder of her nights on the sofa with Nicky, and so she was happy to search out fresh linens and make up three of the upstairs bedrooms. A good night's rest on a comfortable mattress was something she looked forward to, and having Nicky tucked out of the way in his own bed would make it easier to prepare for Santa's visit.

When Marisa finished upstairs, she was careful to take no notice of the foil-wrapped package with her name on it that had appeared beneath the tree, but it was hard not to smile at the smug looks on both Mac's and Nicky's faces.

Nicky was still of an age when the smallest things delighted him, so her worries about disappointing him Christmas morning had subsided, especially after she'd seen the neat job Mac had done on the old sled. Between the things she'd made and the few odds and ends she'd rustled up out of Paul's belongings—a pack of cards, a dozen brand-new colored pencils—she was fairly confident that her son's fifth Christmas would be memorable in its own unique fashion. With a shiver of fear, she also fervently hoped and prayed that it wouldn't be the last one they'd share together.

They spent the remainder of the morning playing numerous games of checkers, making fudge and discussing the menu for the Christmas feast—a challenge, since the pantry lacked the ingredients for a traditional turkey dinner. There was a boisterous debate concerning the various merits of spaghetti over corned beef hash. They adjourned without reaching a consensus, then, as no one was interested in lunch after their huge breakfast and too many samples of chocolate fudge, they bundled up for an outing.

The air was still frigid, but since they'd been cooped up inside under gray skies for several days, the pleasure of feeling the sunshine on one's skin again more than made up for the temperature. With Mac's help, Nicky constructed the "biggest snowman in the whole, wide world." In return, Nicky and his mom carted the firewood Mac had split from the backyard to the pile on the rear veranda. To celebrate a job well done, Marisa taught Nicky how to make snow angels, and after a while there was hardly an untouched drift anywhere around the four sides of the lodge. Finally Marisa had to cry uncle.

"Nicky, please! It's time to go in. Your poor mom is frozen!" After shaking off the snow clinging to her back, Marisa clapped hands and stamped feet to bring life back into her numb extremities. Though his nose was bright red, the boy was typically reluctant to break up the fun. His protest halted her at the bottom of the front porch steps.

"Aw, Mommy! Me and Mac were gonna make another snowman!"

"Yeah, Mom," Mac drawled, grinning. "Don't be a spoilsport."

"Can't you save some fun for tomorrow?" She could see that the boy was tired from all his exertions, but a frontal attack never worked with her stubborn son. She tried a diversionary tactic instead. "You know what? We still haven't hung up a stocking for you—and Santa's coming tonight!"

Nicky's mouth popped open in shock. "That's right!"

"Ooh, you play dirty, don't you, Mom?" Mac accused, his voice low and amused.

"All's fair, Mahoney," she replied airily. "Come along, Nicky."

"We gotta get a big one, Mommy." Nicky's cold-reddened face was earnest. "The biggest one we can find!"

"Maybe you can use one of Mac's." Marisa darted the tall man an impish look, then tugged her son toward the steps. "He's got *really* big feet."

"Them's fightin' words where I come from."

The snowball hit her square in the back. Marisa rounded on her assailant with a mock-ferocious snarl. "Why, you dirty, low-down, back-shooting varmint—take *that!*"

Ducking, Mac laughed and plastered her chest with another well-placed snowball. With a shriek, Marisa launched her own barrage, and within seconds the air was full of missiles. Nicky joined in, pelting both adults with equal delight as the battle ranged over the snowy expanse in front of the lodge.

Darting in and out from behind tree trunks, racing for cover behind bushes, Marisa was laughing so hard she could scarcely aim. Just as Mac was about to close in on her, Nicky went on the counterattack. A lucky hit on the side of Mac's neck sluiced icy slush under his collar, and his yelp of surprise doubled Nicky over with hilarity.

"Turncoat!" Mac hollered, a grin as big as Texas splitting his face. "You'd better watch out—"

"Get him, Nicky!" Marisa yelled, pelting Mac repeatedly.

Arms raised to fend off the hail of snowballs, Mac looked ready to surrender. Then he gave a loud roar, charged straight at Marisa and brought her down with a flying tackle that landed them both in a powdery drift. Nicky jumped up and down, smothering delighted chuckles behind his mittens.

Flat on her back, held down by Mac's superior weight, Marisa gasped and giggled uncontrollably. "You crazy sidewinder!"

Mac's chest shook with laughter. "Don't call the law names, lady. I might have to haul you off to the hoosegow."

"Bully." Dazzled by the halo of sunlight behind his head, she smiled up at him.

"Hellion." He smiled down into her eyes.

"Barbarian." Her smile wavered and her glance settled on his mouth.

"She-devil." His words were husky, hungry.

"Tough guy." Her whisper taunted, invited.

"Wildcat." Playfulness gone, need blazing, Mac covered her mouth with his.

The warmth of his lips was a delicious shock against her cool skin. Heated, her blood steamed through her veins, and her heart, already pounding, tripped over in a new cadence, faster and more reckless than she'd ever experienced.

Mac drew back slowly, his expression watchful, his eyes burning. A pair of five-year-old knees plopped into the snow at Marisa's shoulder. "Mac!" Wonderment colored Nicky's piping words. "Why ya kissin' Mommy?"

Never taking his gaze from Marisa's flushed countenance, Mac said, "Because I like the way she tastes."

Nicky made a face. "Ugh, gross."

"Better look the other way then, because I'm going to do it again."

Before Marisa could frame a coherent protest, he proceeded to do just that, kissing her with such sweetness that he stole her breath and melted her bones. Then he was on his feet and pulling her to hers, steadying her as he dusted the snow from her jacket and adjusted her knit cap around her ears.

"Oh, I get it!" Nicky nodded thoughtfully. "We had a fight. An' we had to kiss and make up!"

Mac's eyes darkened. "Exactly."

His look was so intense Marisa felt it like a caress . . . or a plea. For atonement and forgiveness? She wanted to believe it. Everything in her being hoped that what she was reading in her former lover's expression was an opening, a start at reconciliation. The prospect was as frightening as it was exhilarating.

Nicky stumbled to his feet, his face screwed up in disgust. "Well, I'm not kissing anybody!"

Mac turned his gaze to the boy, and his mouth quirked. "Believe it or not, cowpoke, you won't always want to kiss just your horse."

Rattled more than she wanted to admit, her face still flaming, Marisa reached for her son's hand. "Come on, Nicky. Time to get us both warm and dry."

"And hang my stocking!"

"Right." Licking her lips, Marisa shot Mac a wary glance. He stood with his feet braced apart, his hands jammed in his parka pockets, watching her back. She gulped. "Are you coming?"

"Uh, I think I'll hike down to check on my Jeep."

She frowned. "Is that wise?"

"Maybe not," he muttered. "But, all things considered, at the moment it's safer."

"Oh." His oblique admission that he wanted her struck an answering chord deep in her middle. She knew he was right. "Uh, just watch yourself, okay?"

"Worried about me, princess?" he teased. "Careful, such a show of concern is liable to go straight to my head."

"It would, with your ego, Mahoney," she retorted, turning Nicky toward the lodge. "I just don't want to have to come dig my firewood foreman out of a snowdrift. So don't take any chances, all right?"

"Yes, ma'am." He sketched a mocking salute and started down the roadway.

Uneasiness made her pause halfway up the porch steps and call after him, "Remember it gets dark early."

"Go inside, Marisa." Beneath the hood of his jacket, his expression grew warm with promise. "I'm coming back. You can bank on it."

Throwing her another wave, he headed downhill through the knee-deep snow. Shaken more by what he hadn't said than his actual words, Marisa did as she was told.

While she popped Nicky into a warm bath, she tried to organize her scattered thoughts. Was what she and Mac were experiencing a product of enforced confinement, or might it actually be leading somewhere? They had so much history to work through, regaining their past might never be possible. But that wasn't what she wanted, was it? No, the past was gone and they were no longer the same people they'd been ten years earlier. But had they both grown and changed in ways that might make a serious relationship possible? Certainly the attraction was still as strong as ever.

Persuading Nicky to take a rest after the afternoon's exertions was harder than Marisa expected, especially in her unsettled frame of mind. Finally she lay down with him on his newly made bed and told him the Christmas story, an appropriate way, she thought, of reminding them both of the true reason behind the holiday celebrations. Talk of angels and shepherds and a tiny baby in a manger soon had the little boy drowsy enough to nap, and Marisa stole away, looking forward to a little wicked indulgence of her own.

The hot spray of the shower felt wonderful. For some reason, her skin was sensitized, and the water sluicing down her body was a sensual caress. Suddenly impatient with herself, she grabbed a bottle of shampoo and furiously began to lather her hair. Didn't she have enough trouble without becoming involved again with Mac Mahoney? Just because he still knew how to kiss a woman senseless didn't mean she could forget about why they had both found themselves in this peculiar situation!

After blotting the moisture from her limbs and smoothing on lotion, she donned fresh jeans and a soft cashmere sweater the color of apricots, meanwhile trying to think logically about the emotional intensity that had been growing over the past few days. Circumstances were making her fanciful, that was all, she told herself firmly. The fantasy of being held again, of leaning on someone's strength—just for a little while—was alluring, but she hadn't fought her way to her present success by counting on anyone but herself. Why, then, did she find herself looking out the window for Mac every five minutes?

Wrestling with her disturbed musings, she went downstairs to sit on the stone hearth and brush her hair dry before the fire. She was bent over upside down stroking the last of the moisture from her curls when Mac came through the front entrance.

His face was ruddy with cold and exertion, and his brow was creased with a perplexed frown, as if he was considering something of monumental importance. He hung up his parka and turned just as she straightened, flipping the wild blond mass of her hair back to hang loose over her shoulders. When he saw her, his face cleared, and he smiled.

Marisa felt the breath go out of her with a small "whuff," and froze. She watched helplessly as he crossed to her, then tangled his chilled hands in her hair.

"God, you're so beautiful," he said, and bent to kiss her again. When he drew back, Marisa's lips clung to his shamelessly. The realization was shocking. Forcing her hazy eyes to open took a supreme effort, but she made an attempt to regain control of the situation. "You'd better stop doing that, Mahoney." Strong words; unfortunately her voice held a breathless and very revealing quaver.

"You like it, don't you?" he murmured, rubbing his thumbs over her temples.

"Too much," she admitted. Worry shadowed her eyes to indigo. "But it's not smart right now."

Laughter rumbled in his chest. "You always said I never had a lick of sense."

She caught his wrist and gently disentangled herself. "Try to prove me wrong for once, will you? How's your Jeep?"

He accepted her rebuff with equanimity, straightening to extend his palms toward the fire. "Still in one piece. It'll take some digging out, but I might try driving it up here tomorrow if the weather holds."

"I see." She chewed her lip, realizing that if he was able to move his vehicle, then that would be the first step toward ending their confinement. Her reprieve was coming to an end sooner than she'd hoped. She stood. "Uh, that was quite a hike. Would you like something hot to drink?"

"Sounds good." He followed her into the kitchen. "Hey, what's this?" The package that Nicky had so carefully wrapped in aluminum foil that morning lay open on the kitchen table. The contents were missing. Mac gave a snort of exasperation. "That little dickens! I thought I'd talked him out of the feathers!"

"What feathers?" Marisa demanded.

Mac's expression became mischievous and secretive. "Uh-uh, princess. No questions. Don't want to spoil the little guy's surprise, do you?"

Laughing softly, she put on the kettle and reached for a package of instant hot cocoa mix. "No, of course not. And I want to thank you for helping him, Mac. It's awfully sweet of you."

"Sweet?" He tugged his earlobe, looking a bit sheepish. "Selfish is more like it. It's like . . . like magic, seeing everything through the kid's eyes. I'm really looking forward to playing Santa, you know. It's a new experience for me."

Touched, she smiled at him. "Then I'm glad you're here to share it with us."

"Me, too." They stood watching each other, as awkward as two adolescents, until the kettle's whistle made them jump. Hastily Marisa stirred hot water into the mix and handed Mac the mug. He took a grateful sip, then cleared his throat. "I guess I'd better go see what that rascal of yours wants to do about this present."

"He's napping."

"On Christmas Eve? That's un-American!"

Laughing, she shook her head at his nonsense. "Oh, all right, go wake him up then. It is getting late, and otherwise I'll never get him to sleep tonight at all."

"Fine, I'll do that." Carrying his mug, Mac headed out of the kitchen.

"Soup for supper okay?" she called.

"Fine. Whatever's easy."

Opening cans wasn't exactly the hardest thing in the world, of course. Within a minute, Marisa had prepared condensed vegetable soup and put it on low heat to warm. She was struggling to open a stubborn tin of crackers when Mac reappeared in the kitchen doorway. "I hope Nicky wasn't too grumpy. . . ." Something strange in his expression made her words trail away uncertainly. "Mac? What is it?"

"Nicky's not upstairs."

"What?" She dropped the crackers and came around the counter. "He has to be!"

Mac caught her arm. "Don't panic now. He's around here somewhere."

"Well, of course he is! Nicky! Come out this instant! Honestly, that boy—" Marisa glanced at the back door, then to the empty coat hook beside it. It took her a moment to comprehend what she saw, then she gasped in horror.

Nicky's jacket and boots were missing.

Six

————

"He's not in the garage."

"Did you check the generator room?"

"He's not there, either."

Shivering uncontrollably beneath her ski jacket and knit muffler, Marisa jammed a gloved fist against her mouth to contain a whimper of pure terror.

Nicky was nowhere in the yard or driveway, and the snow at their feet was so chopped up from their earlier play that the footprints of one small, very naughty boy bent on some obscure errand could not be distinguished from the rest of the tracks. Worse than that, lengthening shadows stretched across the landscape, and the first evening star gleamed in the navy blue band of twilight creeping up from the western horizon.

"Where can he be?" Marisa cried. "Nicky!"

"He can't have gone far." Mac's breath made puffs of

white in the frigid air. He laid a reassuring hand on her shoulder. "We'll find him."

"He's lost. Anything could happen! What if he's fallen in a snowdrift where we can't see him? Or the stream? And, oh, God, what about wolves?" Hysteria growing, she flinched from Mac's touch. "It's all your fault. If not for you, we wouldn't even be here!"

"Calm down, Marisa—"

"Don't tell me to calm down! My son's out there! How could I let this happen? How could I be so busy mooning over you that I forget to take care of my baby? Oh, God, I'll never forgive myself—"

"That's enough!" Hands grasping her shoulders, Mac shook her hard. "Snap out of it! You either stay calm enough to help me, or you go inside and wait. I can't waste time mollycoddling a hysterical female. Do you understand me?"

His blunt words were like a dash of cold water, and just what she needed. White-faced, Marisa grabbed on to what was left of her composure and nodded. "Yes."

"All right, then. So Nicky's a little more enterprising than most five-year-olds. My guess is he's after another feather for the earrings we made for your Christmas present."

Her eyes widened. "The bird's nest down in the fir grove?"

"It's worth a try. Come on."

Hurrying, calling, they followed the path left from their tree-cutting expedition down the back slope and into the woods. It was colder there, and gloomier, growing dark so quickly Marisa was afraid they wouldn't be able to see Nicky's tracks even if they stumbled across them.

The fir grove was deserted.

"Oh, God, where else can he be?" Marisa moaned, fighting renewed panic. Her throat was raw with calling, but she tried again. "Nicky!"

"I could have sworn..." Grim-faced, Mac circled the area, his eyes straining at the broken ground for any sign.

"We'll have to go back, start over at the lodge. We may need help...." Marisa's words trailed off and her heart stopped as full cognition of Nicky's dangerous predicament overcame her. The phone lines were dead, and Gwen's midprice car lacked the cellular setup that the Mercedes Marisa had left behind in L.A. boasted. Snow-clogged roads or not, Mac would have to dig his Jeep out and drive into the nearest town. But it would be full dark soon, and even if a search and rescue team could be notified, then placed in the field, a small child might not survive an unprotected night at this altitude and temperature. Desperation laced her voice. "Mac, tell me what to do. I'm so frightened!"

"Here it is!" His elated cry came from behind a heavy-limbed fir whose silhouette resembled an elegant Civil War–period ball gown. "Marisa, quick!" Heart in her throat, she staggered through the stiff snow, and found him on one knee examining an indentation in the icy surface. "He's been here, all right. Looks like the rascal climbed the damn tree and came down this side by mistake." Mac pointed. "That way."

"Oh, thank God!"

"It's getting so dark—" Mac broke off, patted his pockets, then produced a small black penlight. A bright circle illuminated Nicky's footprints. "Why didn't I think of this before? Come on."

Marisa eagerly complied, jogging on his heels as he followed Nicky's trail through the rapidly thickening undergrowth. "What else have you got in all those pockets, Captain Kangaroo?"

Mac hesitated, and when he spoke his tone was light. "Oh, you might be surprised. Rabbits, maybe."

Marisa's voice shook. "I hope you don't have to pull one out of your hat to get us out of this fix."

Mac stopped so abruptly she banged into him. He caught the back of her neck and steadied her, his breath warm in her face, his voice rough. "I'm not going to let anything bad happen to either you or Nicky. You got that, princess?"

Unbelievably, the certainty in his promise eased the tightness in her chest. "Yes, Mac."

"And don't you forget it. Now call your boy." She did as she was told, and Mac added his shouts to hers. Leading the way, Mac pushed aside limbs and held back branches, the thin beam of the penlight never leaving the trail of small bootprints. "Good grief, this kid's a trooper," he muttered. "He's got to sit down and rest sometime—"

"Mac, wait." Marisa caught his sleeve, her head tilted in an attentive attitude.

"What—"

"Shh!" Straining, she listened hard. Like all mothers, recognition of her child's voice was instantaneous. The faintly heard "Mommy" sent a surge of joyous relief through her. She rushed past Mac, stumbling, calling, fighting tears. "Nicky! Don't move! We're coming!"

"Marisa!" Mac charged after her, the flashlight beam stabbing into the darkness ahead. He caught the back of her jacket in his fist to slow her. "Careful!"

But she'd already stopped and was staring in horror down into the blackness filling the precipice at her feet. The illusion was total, for it could have been a drop-off of a foot— or a mile. "Nicky! Where are you?"

His voice came from below. "Mommy, I'm stuck!" Still holding Marisa's jacket, Mac pointed the penlight over the edge. He waved it back and forth until it caught the gleam of a fair head. A bank of raw earth, barely covered by snow, sloped downhill from the drop-off at a forty-five degree angle. The boy sat comfortably about eight feet down, the hem and hood of his red jacket snagged in a nest of bare, protruding roots. It was impossible to know how much farther it was to the bottom—or even if there was a bottom.

Nicky squinted up into the light, tear tracks shimmering on his red cheeks. "Get me loose!"

"I'm coming, partner," Mac said. "Don't move a muscle."

Marisa's teeth chattered. "Mac—"

"Take this." He thrust the penlight into her hand and shrugged out of his parka. In just his shirt, he examined the incline with suspicious eyes. Without warning, he reached and unwrapped Marisa's knitted muffler from her neck and knotted it around his left wrist. Between his six-foot-plus frame and the scarf, he thought he could reach Nicky. "Lifeline," he muttered. "You hold on to this end, okay? I'm going down on my belly."

"Yes." She swallowed. "Be careful."

"Piece of cake." He knelt then dropped his legs over the edge of the drop and began to inch down.

Marisa squatted, aiming the flashlight with one hand and keeping a death grip on the end of the muffler twisted around her wrist. "Nicky, stay right where you are. Mac's coming to get you."

"Okay, Mommy. I went off the path. I didn't mean to. It got dark. Are you mad?"

Mac glanced up and met her gaze. She was amazed to see mischief dancing in his eyes. "Uh—we'll talk about that later, honey. It's time to go home now."

"Here I come, cowpoke." Choosing his handgrips carefully and using his toes to brake his decline, Mac slithered closer to the boy. Marisa lay on her stomach, head and shoulders over the edge, attached to the scene below by the dual umbilical cords of a knitted lifeline and a narrow band of light.

"Do exactly what Mac says, okay?" she pleaded.

"Yes, Mommy."

"Here we go." Digging in the toes of his boots, Mac put one arm around Nicky's middle and jerked on the snagged jacket with his other hand until it tore free. "Now slide over and get in front of me. I'm going to give you a boost to the top."

"Cool." Tongue tucked in the corner of his mouth, Nicky scrambled on all fours up toward his mother while Mac placed a hand on his bottom and pushed.

Marisa stuck the penlight between her teeth and extended her free hand, reaching, reaching... then grabbing a handful of Nicky's jacket. She hauled him over the edge with a strength she hadn't known she possessed and sat him down beside her with a soft thud.

"Whee! That was fun, Mommy. I—"

She whipped the penlight out of her mouth and stuck it in the snow. "Don't talk, young man, and don't move." Marisa's tone was so sharp, Nicky looked up in amazement, but obeyed. Still holding onto the muffler for dear life, she reached back over the edge again for Mac. The thin beam of the flash offered little illumination beyond the drop. "Mac, here."

"I can manage." His dark head bobbed as his toe slipped. With a grunt of surprise, he slid down a foot.

Fear turned her blood to ice. Frantic, she stretched for him. "Mac! *Take—my—hand!*"

Pushing with his feet, he shoved himself upward. He was almost close enough. Their fingers brushed once, missed again, then clasped tightly. Using her support, Mac levered himself over the edge. He fell on his back in the snow, gasping. "Appreciate it."

Marisa laid a hand over his heart for a split second in silent thanks, then pulled Nicky into her arms and crushed him to her. For a moment, they all rested. Then Mac sneezed. Eyes bright, nerves still wound tightly, Marisa became instantly businesslike.

"Lord, what are we doing sitting around in the snow like a bunch of penguins? Mac, hand me my muffler and get that coat back on before you catch your death. Nicky, anything hurt? Can you feel your feet and your fingers?"

"I'm okay, Mommy. Just hungry!"

Cracking orders like a general, Marisa had them on their feet in moments. Parka fastened, Mac hefted Nicky up for a piggyback ride home. Marisa led the way, retracing their path with the aid of the penlight.

"Quite a Christmas Eve jaunt you took, cowpoke," Mac commented.

"I got lost," the boy admitted, clutching Mac's neck.

"The important thing is you didn't panic."

"Oh, no. Mommy told me how to find my way."

Marisa cast a quick glance over her shoulder. "I did? How?"

"Just like in the Christmas story. I followed the star."

"I guess Santa won't come at all now." Nicky sighed.

Mac paused in the process of toweling down the youngster. The bathroom was filled with steamy heat from the shower they'd shared to warm up after their adventure. Hips wrapped in a towel, Mac rubbed the boy's spiky hair, then reamed out his ears for good measure. "How come, partner?"

"I been awful bad today." Nicky's brow puckered with worry as Mac quickly helped him don underwear and a pair of red, white and black footed pajamas.

"You gave your mom a bad scare," Mac acknowledged, picking up another towel and scrubbing his own hair dry. "You know, Nicky, even a cowboy has to take responsibility when it comes to the people who love him."

"Yeah. She's pretty mad, huh?"

"No, not that exactly." Mac pulled on another pair of Paul's disreputable sweatpants and a ragged UCLA sweatshirt, took a swipe with a comb at Nicky's head and then his own, and finally reached for a balled-up pair of athletic socks. "It's just that we have to think twice before we do things, so we don't hurt other people."

Mac felt a peculiar pang at his own words. In his own way, he was as guilty as Nicky—more so, when it came to causing Marisa pain.

The boy sighed again. "It's hard to remember, isn't it?"

"Yeah, and sometimes we think we have good reasons for what we do. Like I know you really wanted to make those earrings special for your mom. Just tell me, did you learn anything from all this?"

"Not to go outside without telling a grown-up 'cause it's dangerous. And kinda scary in the dark, too."

"That's right. Since nobody got hurt, and you learned your lesson, your mom won't stay angry, especially if you tell her you're sorry again."

"I'll tell her a hundred times!"

"Once will be enough." Mac hid a smile. "Let's wrap up her present again and put it under the tree where it belongs. And I bet you can count on old Santa showing up tonight."

"Really?"

"Sure. Now, let's go get our soup. I'm starved, aren't you?"

"Yep!" The boy nodded vigorously, then his blue eyes latched with undisguised longing on to the sock Mac held.

"You never got to hang up your stocking, did you?" Mac asked with sudden insight. "Want to borrow one of these?"

"Yeah! It's humongous!"

Handing over the clean, long cotton sock with the red band at the top, Mac laughed and ruffled Nicky's hair. "Let's do it now, before we eat."

Downstairs, their discussion over the merits of a thumbtack versus a nail as the fastener of choice for Christmas stockings drew Marisa from the kitchen. "What's going on?" She gave Mac's one bare foot a quizzical look.

"All in the name of a good cause," he explained.

Her lips tilted briefly. "Right up your alley."

Mac frowned. Was that the only way she saw him? Busy with a life that revolved around causes and not people?

"I'm going to hang it here, Mommy!" Excited, Nicky stood on the hearth clutching the sock. His expression became suddenly uncertain. "Mac said it was okay. But maybe Santa won't come—"

"Of course he's coming!" Mac saw Marisa swallow. Then she went to help Nicky press the thumbtack through the edge of the sock and into the wooden mantel. "Don't you worry," she said. "He'll find us. After all, that jolly old elf lives at the North Pole! A little snow won't stop him."

Nicky perked up immediately and pushed on the tack with renewed zeal. Then he threw his arms around Marisa's neck. "I love you, Mommy. I'm sorry I scared you."

Ah, you little con-artist! Mac smiled as Marisa melted like butter in her son's embrace. She gathered Nicky close for a huge hug, then sat down on the sofa with him in her lap for a quiet talk.

While Nicky appeared none the worse for wear, Mac knew that despite her smiles Marisa was the one who'd taken the heaviest hit. Fatigue drew the corners of her mouth down when she wasn't making an effort to be cheerful, and shadows still darkened her eyes. Even tired as hell and frazzled to within an inch of her life, she was still as beautiful as an angel. Mac reflected with sympathy that this parenting thing sure took its toll sometimes. Remembering Nicky's affection toward him, he acknowledged that it had its rewards, too.

They ate vegetable soup and crackers, followed by containers of chocolate pudding. Afterward, Mac helped Nicky rewrap his mother's gift, stoked the fire, then found a concert of Christmas music on the television. Slumped in one of the oversize chairs, he propped his feet on the hearth and listened to Marisa's melodious voice as she read bedtime stories to Nicky while traditional carols played in the background.

Before long, the events of the day caught up with the boy, and he lay half-asleep in the crook of his mother's arm. Mac rose and went to them. "Time to tuck the little cowpoke in, I see. I'll carry him up for you."

Somewhat to his surprise, Marisa didn't object as he lifted Nicky, merely followed him up the stairs to the center guest room the boy had chosen between Mac's and hers and pulled back the bed covers. As Mac laid him down, Nicky murmured sleepily, "Mommy, can I get up early to see what Santa brought?"

"As early as you like, darling." Sifting his fair hair between her fingers, she bent to press a kiss to his forehead. "Good night."

"Night." Yawning, the boy snuggled into the covers. "Merry Christmas, Mac."

"Same to you, partner." Mac met Marisa's eyes, and they both smiled. A feeling of closeness and contentment unlike anything he'd ever experienced filled him.

After a few moments, Marisa turned off the bedside lamp and led them out of the room, carefully pulling the door shut.

"What time does Santa usually arrive, anyway?" Mac asked, following her down the staircase. The day's exertions were catching up with him, too, and he rolled his head to release the stiffness in his neck and shoulders. "I want to be there to see the look on Nicky's face."

"Well, he's worn out, so he might sleep all the way to six o'clock." She shot him a wry look. "Or then again, maybe not. Last year it was two-thirty in the morning."

"Good grief!"

"I never know. That's why it's best to set out things just as soon as he goes to sleep."

"You're the boss, Mom. I'll go get the sled."

A short while later, Marisa looked up from stuffing an assortment of objects into the white sock, and her eyes went round with pleasure at the bright red sled Mac carried into the den. He'd even added a new nylon towrope he'd rescued from an old tent. "Oh, Mac, it's beautiful! Thank you. He's going to love it."

"Think so?"

"I know so. Put it here beside the chair."

Mac propped the newly refurbished sled at the foot of the easy chair, admiring the arrangement of a button-eyed stick horse and a miniature pair of cowboy chaps any boy would be proud to wear. Marisa rose and laid the now-knobby sock in the seat between them, then added a big red cloth bow to the arrangement.

"It's all in the presentation," she confided, looking at the pile with a critical eye and adjusting the angle of the stick horse.

"I hope the little fellow isn't pining for something that's not here. I remember once I wanted this dragline..."

"He'll be too thrilled with all these surprises to miss anything. And besides, I've wrapped up a little box with an I.O.U. from Santa for an all-expense-paid shopping trip to the toy store at a later date."

"Instead of a rain check, a snow check?"

She smiled. "Exactly."

"That's using the old noggin."

"Being a parent keeps you creative." Her light tone faltered and her lip trembled. With a shaking hand, she made another minute adjustment to the stocking. "I could have lost him, Mac."

He placed a hand on her nape and massaged her tense muscles. "Hey, you didn't. Concentrate on that. And in the morning, you'll spend Christmas together—"

"But what about next Christmas? What if I lose him in a completely different way?"

Guilt swamped Mac. He was responsible for precipitating the events that not only had led to Nicky's misadventure, but would also perhaps lead to his being reunited with his birth mother. Four days earlier, he would have shrugged it off, said it was justice done and forgotten about it, but he'd seen what being a family meant, and now the dilemma tore at him. He dropped his hand. "Marisa, I don't know what to say."

"Then don't say anything. Just listen. I want to apologize."

"For what?"

"I said some pretty harsh things out there this afternoon. I just want you to know that I didn't mean them, and I'm sorry." Biting her lip, she looked up at him. "Thank God you were here, Mac. I couldn't have found Nicky alone. I wouldn't have known what to do on that slope."

"Sure you would have," he contradicted. "In the past few days I've learned that you're a woman capable of just about anything—uncommon fortitude, determination, drive. You'd have done what you had to do."

"I'm just glad it didn't come to that. You did something very special for me and at great risk to yourself. I'll never forget that. Thank you for being there."

He felt a bit sheepish at such high praise. "Hey, it was nothing."

"Not to me." Her mouth trembled, and she blinked furiously, losing the fight as a tear spilled over her lashes and trickled down her cheek. "Oh, God, Mac. You can't know how it feels when you think you've lost someone you love."

Something hit him in the chest, and his throat constricted. "I know exactly how it feels—I lost you, didn't I?"

For an instant, neither one moved. Then Marisa gave a little helpless murmur and reached for him, and suddenly he held her in his arms, crushing her sweet length to him, burying his face in the fragrant curve of her neck.

She sobbed against his collarbone. "I'm sorry, Mac. I'm sorry."

"Don't." He tightened his grip, feeling the betraying moisture slide from the corners of his own eyes. "Marisa, don't."

Her fingers were on his face, and he was revealed to her. It didn't seem to matter. "I'm . . . sorry," she repeated brokenly. "I—I know I hurt you. But I hurt myself more."

"No more blame. Maybe we were both too young, too careless to know what we had."

"I knew," she said, lifting a face streaked with tears. She trailed her lips along his jawbone until he turned his mouth to hers. "I knew, and I never forgot."

Groaning, Mac could do nothing but accept her invitation. Slanting his mouth across hers, he kissed her, losing himself in her taste, shaking in every fiber as he felt her trembling against him. Her arms went around his neck, and her fingers delved into his hair as she pulled him closer with a need that inflamed him.

Nimble tongues twined in a mating both primitive and powerful as their bodies strained together in erotic mimicry. Fire shot through Mac's bloodstream and lodged low and aching in his loins. Without volition, his hand crept beneath her sweater, and he cupped her full breast, reveling in the seductive softness of her. She moaned against his mouth. Using the last of his self-control, he pulled back, his breathing heavy. "You're killing me, you know that?"

Her eyes were dazed and heavy lidded, and her breathing was no steadier than his own. "Then let's die together."

His hands tightened on her, and his voice was hoarse. "You don't offer a starving man a tidbit, Marisa. And, uh, I'm not prepared—"

"Don't worry, the timing isn't right. I haven't been with anyone since Victor died, and I assume you had a physical the last time you went abroad."

"Uh, yeah. Not that there's been anyone special in a long time for me, either. But you'd better be sure—"

"I need you," she whispered. "I need *us*. Oh, Mac, it's been so long . . . I've missed you so much."

Her raw admission absolved him, released him of the necessity of any control, freed him to assuage the hunger that burned in his belly. Feeling savage, he took her mouth again. Ruthlessly tender, tenderly untamed, he drank from her over and over like a man who'd been lost in the desert and had suddenly stumbled upon the sweetest, most refreshing fountain on earth.

She was no less greedy, straining against him, opening her mouth for his invasion, then parrying with her own erotic thrusts, driving him mad with desire. Growling in his throat, he reached for her sweater, lifting it and her chemise over her head in one movement to reveal the creamy perfection of her breasts.

Her hands were no less demanding, struggling with his sweatshirt until he threw it off, too. She lightly traced the half-healed bruise on his shoulder, then ran her fingers through his chest hair to tarry on the flat bronze coins of his nipples. Mac started at her teasing touch and cupped her pale shoulders in his large palms. He found himself trembling at the delicacy of her bones, the smoothness of her skin.

She was everything he'd remembered, everything he'd dreamed of through ten long and lonely years, and so much more—womanly and enticing and modest and proud all at once. And he wanted her with a boundless passion that he'd never imagined he could recapture. He nibbled her earlobe, then let his teeth gently score her collarbone. He smiled as she quaked in his arms, and when he set his lips on the crown of her nipple, she nearly came apart.

She bent over him, cupping his cheeks with her palms, tracing the play of muscles as he licked and suckled, coercing the tips into tight buds, the sweetest flesh in the world to him. The curtain of her hair washed over his shoulders, touching his bare skin with pale fire. "Mac..." Her voice was an ache.

"I know, honey. I know." He touched the tip of his tongue to the center of her breastbone, then knelt and trailed kisses down her stomach. Quickly he unzipped the fly of her jeans, cupped her slender waist and pushed his tongue into the indentation of her navel.

Swaying, her fingers twisting in his hair, she gasped. "You are a wicked, wicked man, Mahoney."

Smiling, he pushed her jeans down her legs. Moving his mouth to settle over the silk-covered apex of her thighs, he inhaled the still-familiar scent of womanly musk and arousal that would always be uniquely Marisa to him. His fingers slid beneath the elastic of her bikini briefs and he palmed her buttocks, holding her still for his attentions, allowing no demur, no refusal, until she was all but sobbing.

"Mac..." Her hands clenched in his hair, she urged him to his feet. He slipped off her shoes and pushed all of her clothing free, then stood, intending to lift her into his arms to carry her upstairs.

He hadn't counted on her retaliation.

Kissing him, licking at the hints of her own essence still clinging to his lips, she went on the attack. She slid her hands beneath the elastic waistband of his sweatpants and pushed them down as she smoothed the flat, muscular angles of his buttocks and lean thighs, then rode his hipbones forward to boldly stroke his arousal. Mac felt as though the floor was buckling. "You play dirty," he groaned.

"All's fair, Mahoney." Hands still busy, she used her foot to drag his baggy pants down even farther.

"Yeah?" Groaning again, he caught her hands, pulled them to his mouth and kissed her fingers. "Watch out, lady, or you're liable to get more than you bargained for."

Rubbing herself sinuously against him, she looped her arms around his neck and purred, "Oh, I'm counting on it."

They didn't make it to a bedroom.

They didn't even make it to the sofa.

Bearing her down to the carpet before the hearth, Mac pressed her knees apart, palmed her bottom and buried himself in her heat. She was tight, slick with desire, sheathing him perfectly. He pressed his open mouth to her neck with a sob of pure pleasure. If the earth had opened and swallowed him at that moment, he would have died a happy man.

Marisa clutched at his broad back and locked her heels around his calves, quivering inside and out. When he turned his mouth to hers again, she welcomed him, just as her body had, kissing him with the passion of a woman reborn, writhing against him in need and invitation and longing.

He knew nothing of control or discipline then, only the overpowering need to bury himself in her, to make her his— at least for a time. Moving slowly, he drew back, then surged with a powerful thrust that made her arch and gasp beneath him. Over and over, in a rhythm as ancient as the tides, he took her closer and closer to the brink of ecstasy, until she was frantic, demanding all of him, urging him closer than mere flesh could ever hope to come with her lips and nails and all of her being, everything that was in her spirit.

And then she exploded in his arms with a high, wild cry, shivering and bucking, crying out his name as the paroxysms flooded her. Mac watched the emotion play across her flushed features, both satisfied and aroused to an even higher pitch by the vision of what he—only he—could make her feel.

Lacing his fingers between hers, he held her hands at the sides of her head, lifting himself to see the place where they joined, marveling in the miracle of two made one. Her fingers clenched between his as she came back from the far place where she'd journeyed, and she opened her eyes, staring up into his face in wonder.

"You won't forget this," he said.

Her voice was the barest whisper. "No. Never."

"Good."

Then he began again, driving her to heights she'd never dreamed existed, and taking himself there, too. And when he felt her small shudders of pleasure overtake her again, he let himself follow her this time and plunged over the precipice in a shower of light and fire that seared and cauterized and, finally, healed.

Seven

"Saint Nick is going to get quite a shock if we don't move soon."

"Mmm-hmm." Mac's mouth rested on Marisa's temple, his body still covering hers. The coals in the fireplace shifted. He didn't.

Lovingly she rubbed her hand down the indentation of his bare spine as far as she could reach. "Uh, Mahoney? Don't you find it rather drafty?"

"The least of my worries," he mumbled.

"Which are?"

"Mainly, how I'm going to get you upstairs to a real bed before I'm forced to make love to you again."

Marisa sucked in a tiny breath—thrilled, confused, joyous—because there didn't seem to be words to describe how she felt being held so intimately by the man she loved.

Had never stopped loving.

Would always love.

She stroked Mac's cheek, tenderness and revelation spilling through her in equal parts. She saw it all so clearly now, how her hostility had been born of an instinctual knowledge that she had no defenses where Mac Mahoney was concerned, that down deep she'd known it would end up like this again. Everything he was—strength and hidden vulnerabilities, honor and solitariness—touched chords within her deepest soul, and she was helpless to resist him, for that would be as unthinkable as denying her very self.

And that's what she'd been trying to do all these years. Even her relationship with the man she'd eventually married had been colored by that struggle. Perhaps she and Victor might have overcome it had he lived. That she would never know was a regret she'd always feel.

Closing her eyes, Marisa breathed softly, knowing the mistakes of the past could not be undone. But the future was unwritten, and the things she'd learned about Mac these past days gave her hope. They'd both made mistakes before, but she'd been a girl then, inexperienced and overwhelmed by his masculinity. She was a woman now, tempered by time and adversity, strong enough to fight for what she wanted.

And what she wanted more than anything was to share her life with the man she loved. Despite everything, there had to be a way, and she *would* find it. It was a Christmas promise to herself.

"You're cold." Feeling her shiver, Mac drew away a little.

"On the contrary, I'm quite . . . flushed."

"I'll say. Hot. Heated. Cookin'."

She touched his hair, and her voice was soft. "I didn't notice you complaining."

"A fool I'm not." Mac gazed down into her eyes, and his half smile faded. "It should be awkward, shouldn't it?"

"Not for us."

"Still, after all this time—I'm surprised."

She crooked her arm around his neck, brought his mouth down to hers again and whispered, "I'm not."

Kissing Mac was an ever-unfolding adventure in sensation. His lips were warm, mobile, lazily sampling everything she offered. He rolled to a sitting position, then dragged her across his lap. When he raised his head, his voice was ragged. "Marisa, I don't know where this is going."

Since she had no doubt where she wanted things to lead between them, that hurt. She slid from his grasp then, and he let her go. Unashamed in her nakedness, her body a play of light and shadow in the fire's orangy glow, she began to gather up their clothing. "I never knew you to be so faint-hearted, Mahoney."

He came to his feet, dragged his sweatpants back into place and muttered, "Yeah, well, some things scare the hell out of me."

It was an admission she'd never thought she would hear from him, of all men. In her heart, she knew it was a step in the right direction. Smiling, clothes bundled at her side, she caught his hand and brushed his knuckles over her breast, tormenting them both as her nipple puckered. "I'm not so scary, once you get to know me."

"Marisa..." His warning held a strangled note.

She let him go, tilting her chin, giving him a veiled look through her lashes. "Think about it."

Then she turned and went upstairs, smiling to herself at not only his stupefied expression, but also at the image of what he must be seeing as she mounted those stairs in a kind of reverse striptease. It made her feel sexy and seductive and powerful.

She was not the least bit surprised when some minutes later he pushed open the door to her room, but she could

have laughed at the incredulity on his face when he found
her sitting crossed-legged in the middle of the bed, fresh
sheets pulled invitingly back, waiting for him. "About
time," she pouted, naked and magnificent. She was rewarded by the ruddy flush that mounted his cheekbones and
the emerald flare of desire in his eyes.

"Woman, you play a dangerous game."

"The only kind worth playing, as you well know." Lying
back against the pillows, she laughed softly, her own anticipation rising as surely as the visible leap of his body. "And,
Mac? Lock the door behind you."

"Has he been here?"

"Uh-huh! Hurry, you gotta see!" Nicky said.

Disturbed by the hushed murmurs filtering into his sleepy
brain, Mac reached automatically for the woman beside
him—and came up empty-handed. Frowning, he fought for
consciousness through the lethargy of utter relaxation and
total well-being, annoyed that Marisa wasn't where she
should be, but smiling at the memory of passion shared
throughout a long winter's night. Pulling her empty pillow
to him, he breathed in the scent of her perfume lingering on
the linens. Incredibly, hunger for her began to build again.

"Go on down, honey. We'll be right there." Marisa's
voice came from outside the bedroom door, followed by the
thudding of small pajama-shod feet hotfooting it down the
stairs. Playing possum, Mac felt her presence at the bedside, then her hand on his shoulder. "Mac, wake up. Santa
came."

He caught her around the waist, then rolled her beneath
him. *He's not the only one.* He smiled to himself.

Hair spread like sunlight, eyes open wide and a tide of
pink staining her cheekbones, she gave a breathless laugh.

"You know, Mac, if word got out about what a marsh-mallow you really are, you'd be forever doomed to fluff pieces."

He shuddered. "Don't even think it."

"Your secret's safe with me." Laughing, her eyes spar-kling, she teased, "As long as you do exactly as I say."

"I'm not so sure I like the sound of that."

Her gaze drifted to his mouth. "I can think of one or two suggestions that you might not object to."

He felt a surge of pressure in his loins. "Me, too."

Still laughing, she dodged his assault on her lips. "But not now! Nicky's waiting. We've got to go see what Santa brought."

"I've already had my Christmas present."

Her expression softened to tenderness, and she raised her head to place a soft kiss on his mouth. "So have I." Then she pushed him away and came to her feet, straightening a rumpled chenille housecoat. "But Nicky hasn't. Come on, slowpoke! You said you wanted to watch."

"Wouldn't miss it." Mac sat on the side of the bed, scrubbed a hand down his stubbled jaw and yawned. "What time is, anyway?"

"Almost five-thirty." Laughing at his groan, she went to the door, then gave him a diffident look over her shoulder. "I'll go ahead. If Nicky knew you spent the night in my room . . . well, he might not understand."

Something knotted in Mac's gut. While he might not have any answers yet, the ramifications of the renewal of their relationship—even temporarily—could not be overlooked, nor allowed to confuse an innocent kid. "Sure. I'll be right there."

"Thanks."

Pulling on his clothes, Mac scowled to himself, unwilling to question his own motives too closely and unable to discern even the most rudimentary glimmer of what the future might hold. From the way they'd gone up in flames, it was obvious that he and Marisa had both needed a release from the sexual tension that had built to the combustion point over the past days, even over the past decade. Their compatibility could not be denied. But what did she really want? Hell, what did he want—besides another chance to hold her?

He stopped off in the bathroom to splash cold water on his face, then stood staring at the bleary-eyed man in the mirror. It was more than just great sex, he was sure of that. But had anything fundamentally changed between them? Or would they wake up tomorrow to find that all of this had been just a lovely, erotic Christmas dream?

Mac cursed softly, then slammed out of the bathroom and headed for the stairs. He was damned if he knew what to think, but for once he was just going to let questions lie unanswered—at least for today—and enjoy a little unexpected happiness. God knew he'd had few enough opportunities for that in his life, and only a fool would reject so precious a gift.

"Mac! Come see what Santa brought me!" Bright-eyed, bouncing from foot to foot in his excitement, Nicky rushed to the bottom of the steps, grabbed Mac's hand and dragged him into the den. "You gotta see this!"

"Whoa, cowpoke. What's got you so fired up? Is it Christmas or something?"

"Yeah! And look!" Nicky plopped himself down on the sled and grabbed the rope handle. His tone was full of wonder. "A sled. A real snow sled. And it's even *red!* Just what I've been wanting and wanting! How did Santa know?"

"He's got his ways." Smiling, pleased as punch that Nicky really liked what he'd done to the old sled, Mac sat down on the sofa beside Marisa and laid his arm around her shoulder. She snuggled satisfyingly close and placed her hand on his thigh.

Nicky went "boogity-boogity" on his bottom, then turned pleading eyes at the two adults. "Can I try it out right now? Please?"

"It's not even really daylight yet!" Marisa protested with a laugh.

"But Mommy—"

"Look, sport, after breakfast we'll give it a real shake-down run, see how fast it will go," Mac offered. "Sound good?"

"Promise?"

"Absolutely. In the meantime, what else have you got there?"

"A horse! Watch me!" Distracted, Nicky jumped off the sled, mounted the stick horse and started giddapping and galloping in circles around the sofa.

"A mighty steed as fast as lightning, eh?"

"Yeah, lightning! That's what I'm gonna call him, too—Lightning. And look!" Nicky pounced on the cowboy chaps and carried them to his mother. "Look, Mommy! Just like the real cowboys wear. Help me put them on?"

"Sure, sweetheart." Marisa bent over to adjust the chaps around Nicky's waist and tie the rawhide strips in place over his pajamas. "My, that looks mighty fine, Tex."

"Giddap, Lightning!" Beaming, Nicky made another loop around the den.

Mac smiled, warmed through and through by the child's delight. "It's really magical for him."

Marisa glanced up. "You didn't have much of this kind of thing growing up, did you?"

"Times were hard." He shrugged. "Don't go getting maudlin on my account. My mother did the best she could."

"I'm sure she did. She loved you, or she wouldn't have worked so hard. But someone of your imagination needs more than just bread on the table to survive."

"Yeah? Like what?"

"Make-believe. Fairy tales. Whimsy. Laughter. Love." She tapped his temple with her fingertip. "Fodder for that fertile brain of yours, Mahoney."

His gaze heated. "I believe what I'm imagining right now could get us both arrested."

"Hopeless," she said, laughing. She kissed him lightly and got up. "Completely hopeless, that's what you are. How about some coffee while Nicky unpacks that humongous stocking?"

"Sounds good." He stretched his arms over the back of the sofa, admiring her rumpled and well-kissed appearance. There were patches along her jawline where his beard had abraded her tender skin. It made him feel rather primitive to know that his possession had marked her as completely his. Something in his expression must have made that clear, because she gulped suddenly and blushed, and her lips parted.

"I—I'll get that coffee."

Mac watched her go, grinning. She might have plied her womanly wiles with amazing skill, but she was just as susceptible to him as he was to her. It boded well.

"Look, Mac. Santa stuffed it full!" Jubilant, Nicky lifted the knobby sock and dumped its treasures on the sofa beside Mac.

They admired the spoils over juice, coffee and a stack of toast and jelly and munched away while "toasting" the pencils and cards, apples and chocolate kisses, erasers and transparent tape. Nicky insisted on trying out the colored pencils at once. As the day grew to full light, Mac and Marisa savored their second cups of coffee while Nicky sat at their feet scribbling pictures of cowboys and horses that strangely resembled dinosaurs.

Nicky finally grew tired of his artistic endeavors and climbed into Marisa's lap. "Can we open your presents under the tree now, Mommy?"

"Don't you want to save that until after Christmas dinner?" she teased.

"Aw, Mom!"

Relenting, she shooed him toward the giant tree. "Go get them, then."

"Awright!" Nicky returned momentarily with an armload of oddly wrapped packages. "Yours first, Mommy. Open the one I gave you first!"

She caught Mac's eye over the boy's fair head, and he nodded encouragement to her, understanding the pang she must feel knowing this gift had almost cost her Nicky. Carefully she unfolded the aluminum foil, made the proper exclamations of pleasure, then pulled her son close for a thank-you hug. "They're the most beautiful earrings I've ever seen!"

"Me and Mac made 'em," Nicky said proudly.

"How clever of you." Marisa held them up, smiling at the exotic arrangement of wire, acorn caps and feathers. "You should go into the jewelry business together. I love them!"

"Put 'em on!" Nicky ordered.

Marisa complied, threaded the wire hooks through her ears, then shook her head to make them swing above her shoulders. "They make me feel positively . . . pagan."

"And I have a sudden wild urge to give a Tarzan yell." Mac's grin grew larger as she blushed again.

"Now give her yours, Mac," Nicky urged, sorting another small package out of the pile and pushing it into Mac's hands. "Go on."

Suddenly self-conscious, wondering what he'd been thinking when he decided to do this, Mac handed the little package to Marisa. "Merry Christmas."

"Why, thank you, Mac." Curious, she opened the gift, then sat staring, robbed of all speech.

"What's the matter, Mommy? Don't you like them?"

"Of course I do, honey." Coming out of her daze, she showed off a second pair of earrings, these made of small coins hand-punched to receive the necessary wire. She met Mac's eyes, and he knew that she remembered another time, another gift, too. "I have a similar pair, and they're my favorites. What are these, Mac? Norwegian?"

"Swedish kronor. I guess I left them in my jacket from the last time I passed through Stockholm."

"Your coat-of-many-pockets continues to come in handy." Her lips trembled. "It's very sweet of you. To remember."

Mac threaded his fingers in hers. "I couldn't forget, either."

"Mac next!" Nicky brought a flat, newspaper-wrapped article and thrust it at the man. "I made it myself."

"Hey, you shouldn't have." Mac removed the paper to reveal a foil-covered star emblazoned with the legend, Sheriff Mac.

"Mommy helped me spell the words, but I wrote it myself," Nicky stated proudly. "Aren't you going to pin it on? Mommy says every good guy's gotta have a star."

"I'd be proud to wear it." Mac found that his voice was suspiciously thick. To cover the swell of unexpected emotion, he pinned the star on his sweatshirt, then grabbed Nicky in a bear hug. "Thanks, partner. And there's something there for you from me."

"This one?" Nicky ripped open the paper and held up a small block of translucent material. "What is it?"

"Southern California kids," Mac said in mock disgust. "That's wax for rubbing on your sled runners. This stuff will make it go like crazy!"

"Yeah?" Nicky's eyes widened. "Awesome! Let's try it."

"Later, honey." Marisa pointed. "That gift's for you, too."

"From you, Mommy?"

"Yes, from me. And will you hand Mac that other one?" Nicky passed Mac the present she indicated, then tore into a heavy box from his mother that contained a measuring tape, a block of wood, an assortment of nails and a real hammer. "But only hammer on the board, okay?" Marisa said as they exchanged more hugs. "Uncle Paul wouldn't like to find nails in his lodge that don't belong."

"Neato! Gee, this is the best Christmas I ever had!" The boy immediately set the wood block on the hearth and tried his hand at carpentry.

"You like to live dangerously, don't you, princess?" Mac asked, eyeing Nicky dubiously.

"As long as he follows the rules, we'll be all right."

"As a professional rulebreaker myself, I wouldn't set much store in that."

"I'll keep it in mind. Aren't you going to open your package?"

Hefting the gift, he felt the outline of a book and cocked an inquiring eyebrow at her. "Something edifying, I hope?"

"See for yourself."

He tore off the paper to find a volume of Shel Silverstein's offbeat poetry. "Er, thank you. Interesting choice."

"It's a favorite of Nicky's, but we both thought you should have it, seeing as how you're underprivileged in the silliness department."

"Me?"

"Yes, you. Besides, you'll get a kick out of the poems, and the drawings, too. They're just cracked enough to suit your twisted sense of humor."

"Aren't I a little old for that?"

Her look was arch. "After last night's performance, I can personally testify that, despite a tendency to sometimes take things too seriously, you are far from ancient."

"Thank you very much."

She laughed at his wry expression. "Really, you need to lighten up sometimes, Mahoney." She leaned closer and murmured against his lips, "You can't spend all your time slaying dragons, you know."

Groaning, he pulled her tight against him with one arm and slanted his mouth over hers. As he drew away again, his breathing was gusty. "You're absolutely right. Any chance of adjourning this discussion to a more private location?"

"Maybe." She twiddled with his sheriff's star. "At nap time."

Nibbling at her ear, he murmured, "How many naps does Nicky take a day, anyway?"

Her color high, her eyes bright with passion and promise, Marisa gave him a wicked smile. "Not nearly enough."

"Are you sure he's ready?"

"Trust me."

"But, Mac, he's so young—"

"Gotta let the baby bird fly sometimes, princess. You don't want him growing up a wimp."

"It's another man thing, huh?"

"You got it."

Marisa twisted her gloved hands together, chewed her lip, then nodded. "Not that I understand, but you're the expert . . . so, okay."

"Don't worry, he'll be fine." Mac gestured to the boy perched on his bright red sled at the top of a medium-size hill. "Okay, partner, let 'er rip!"

To Marisa, standing at the bottom, the incline seemed as tall as Mount Everest. Although the bright sun had warmed the Christmas Day air considerably, she shivered with dread as her child prepared to make his first solo sled run.

"Just push off like I showed you, Nicky," Mac shouted, waving. "You can do it. Come on!"

Nicky waved back, dug in his heels and pushed the sled over the edge. Then he was swooping down the hillside, yelling at the top of his lungs in pure delight, carving a picture-perfect track on the slope and sliding to an easy three-point landing right at his mother's feet. "I did it, I did it!" With a hop, he was off the sled and executing a triumphant war dance, which ended with an athlete's gesture—outstretched fist grabbing air and pulling it to his waist—and a satisfied "Yes!"

"You did! Oh, Mac, he really did it!" Marisa was almost as excited, or perhaps relieved that, despite her mother's worries, no disaster had occurred. Jubilant, she hugged her son, then Mac. "That was great!"

"Didn't I tell you?" Mac's grin was unrestrained.

As proud as a new father, came the unbidden thought. Marisa felt a pang for all the years they'd missed together, the children they might have had by this time. But regrets were useless, and the triumphs of the day were sufficient— Mac's loving, the warm family holiday they were making for Nicky, the screaming, shrieking fun they'd had plummeting down the hill all morning.

Watching Mac give Nicky fresh instructions and tips for the next run, Marisa felt her heart swell with hope and love. No man could experience all this genuine warmth without being affected. It had to mean something to him. It had to!

Mac stepped back to watch Nicky trudge up the hill again, dragging the sled. "The kid's a natural. Great instincts. Great hands. The track's getting sluggish, though. Have you noticed? Sun's melting the crust."

At his words, Marisa suddenly became conscious of a barely audible drip-drip-drip. Water droplets seeping from the underside of branches and plopping against the softening snow sounded a death knell for their snowbound sanctuary. The outside world would intrude whether she liked it or not, and whether she was ready or not to face the consequences of disappearing, as well as the realities of what the Dr. Franco Morris affair and Elsie Powers's claim meant for her future and Nicky's.

She licked dry lips and swallowed. "I suppose you'll move your Jeep now."

Mac turned to look at her, his expression shuttered. After a moment, he shrugged and shifted his gaze back to the small figure in the red jacket climbing the hill. "It'll wait."

Relief and pleasure and hope ran through her veins like warm honey, and she smiled. "All this sledding has made me hungry! I'm going in to work on our Christmas dinner, okay?"

"What? And leave your youngster in my nefarious clutches?"

"All this male bonding is good for him. Besides, I trust you." She laughed at his startled look. "I'll call when our holiday feast is ready. Prepare to be dazzled!"

If not dazzled, the two menfolk who arrived, red cheeked and tired, but in excellent spirits, at the Christmas board were at least amazed.

"Pizza?" Mac quizzed.

"And why not?" Nose in the air, waving the round-wheeled pizza cutter like a scepter, Marisa was as haughty as a queen—or at least a princess. "Can't I decree a new holiday tradition—even if it is out of a box?"

"Yeah!" Nicky crowed. "Pizza!"

"Plain cheese for the crown prince of Heartbreak Hill," she said, gesturing them to their chairs. "And sweep-the-kitchen for his lowly subjects."

"Is that a cocktail onion?" Mac demanded, poking suspiciously at a slice. "And smoked salmon?"

"Hey, I had to improvise."

"Yeah, well, you're going to be improvising a bicarb chaser for me if I eat that."

"This from the man who interviewed a psychotic kidnapper at gunpoint? A Middle-Eastern dictator in his own den? A billionaire tax dodger from her mink-lined cell?"

Mac's slow grin crinkled his eyes, and satisfaction laced his voice. "Kept track of me, did you?"

Marisa felt revealing color stain her cheeks as her teasing boomeranged. "I might have, uh, heard something once in a while, naturally. Nicky, will you say grace for us?" She was thankful that Mac allowed her distraction to work and bowed his head with them as Nicky gave thanks. Then, despite his protests to the contrary, he dug into Marisa's innovative pizza with a hearty appetite. By the time they finished, the early morning and strenuous exercise had Nicky yawning and knuckling his eyes.

"Why don't you get him settled?" Mac suggested, pushing away his empty plate. "I'll clean up."

"You? Do dishes?" She let her eyes go wide as she urged Nicky to his feet. "You really do know how to push a woman's buttons, don't you, Mahoney?"

"I can but try." He winked at her, then mouthed the word "Hurry."

Marisa's heart skipped a beat, and anticipation rushed through her veins. It really was a scandal what the man could do to her with a single glance. But when she looked at her sleepy son, she felt so guilty about her impatience that she took extra time reading a story to Nicky and seeing him sound asleep before she closed his door and went back downstairs.

The den was quiet; the kitchen spotless but deserted. Her disappointment was acute, and the strength of her reaction annoyed her. It could be dangerous to become a slave to her fascination with this man, she knew. But rational thought meant nothing in the face of the love and need that filled her. That knowledge made her voice sharper than she intended when Mac came through the back door moments later. "Where were you?"

He slung his parka on a hook and kicked off his boots. "I had to attend to a few chores. Miss me?"

"Don't be ridiculous. But you might have said something...." She knew she sounded petulant, and she didn't like it. "Sorry, Mac, I didn't mean—"

His hands grasping her shoulders, he crowded her against the edge of the table, then ran his lips over the curve of her ear. "My mistake. Forgive me? I shouldn't have kept an eager lady waiting."

She was melting as surely as the ice and snow outside, heated by warm shivers coursing over her skin as he grazed down her neck. "You—you take a lot for granted, Mahoney. Maybe I just wanted to talk."

"Uh-huh. And maybe they'll move the Eiffel Tower to Idaho Falls."

"It's possible. The *Queen Mary* came to Long Beach, California." She arched her neck and closed her eyes. When he opened the buttons of her shirt and slipped his hand inside, she couldn't stifle a low moan of pleasure.

"So talk," he taunted, gently rubbing his thumb over her nipple. "If you can."

"You don't play fair," she panted, plucking at his shirt. "Let's go upstairs."

"Too late." He unsnapped her jeans.

Marisa's eyes flew open. His face was a study in pure male intent, the skin stretched tight over his cheekbones in arousal. Alarm and excitement danced down her spine. "Mac, what—"

"I can't take it slow." Hands sure and purposeful, he bent and stripped her out of her jeans and panties, then lifted her to the tabletop.

Marisa braced her hands on his shoulders. Her belly tightened, and her voice was ragged with desire. "You're out of your mind."

"Clearly, I am," he said, opening his jeans. He positioned himself and eased into her. She was wet and ready, and they both groaned. Mac captured her mouth then, and his tongue took possession as surely as the rest of him. Marisa whimpered, wrapped her arms around his shoulders, held on as he pushed her flat against the tabletop. Overwhelmed, mastered, she had no option but to surrender. She did so gladly, joyously, reaching and stretching, trying to pull him even closer.

She climaxed almost immediately, her scream muffled against his mouth. Mac gave a powerful thrust, and his body tensed and shuddered with the exquisite contractions of his own release.

Still joined, both astonished and sated, they lay unmoving as aftershocks quivered through them. Finally Mac raised his head. His smile was crooked and his breathing unsteady. "I agree with Nicky. This is the best Christmas I ever had!"

Laughing, she tightened her arms around his neck. "Mahoney, you ain't seen nuthin' yet!"

Eight

"**W**ere you really mooning over me?"

Up to her neck in bathtub bubbles, Marisa opened one eye. "Hmm? When?"

"The other day. When Nicky got lost." Mac leaned against the edge of the sink, admiring the view. It was very late—or early, depending on one's perspective—but when he'd roused himself sufficiently to realize Marisa was no longer in bed beside him, he'd had to search her out. The scenery was definitely worth the trip. He'd forgotten the easy intimacy of living with a woman, how seductive it was, how surely a man could be captivated.

"Oh." Languid from an afternoon tryst and hours of late-night loving following Nicky's bedtime, she raised a slender leg and frowned as she watched the suds trail downward. Her hair was pinned up in a haphazard topknot, and bathwater lapped beguilingly at her breasts. "I suppose I may have been ... distracted."

He hitched up the waistband of his sweatpants. "You had a lot on your mind."

"Uh-huh."

"Me, for instance?"

"You, for instance. What is this, Mahoney? Does your ego need stroking? Considering that you've thoroughly ravished me at every opportunity since then, I think you know the answer to your question."

"When a man gets lucky, he can't help but wonder."

She was using a washcloth to scrub suds off her arms, and a crease appeared between her brows. "Wonder what?"

"If his luck is going to hold," he said and knelt beside the tub. He dipped his hand into the tepid water and let the drops fall over the swell of her breast. The liquid made trails though the suds to uncover the rosy crest. It immediately became erect.

"Do you want it to?" Her voice was husky.

"It's a powerfully pleasant experience, ma'am." He let more drops dribble from his fingertips, feeding his own burgeoning response.

"Yes."

"Addicting."

"I agree."

"Clouds a man's poor feeble mind."

She smiled, a sultry look that revealed her pleasure at that admission. "As it should."

"Might make him forget it can't last."

"You sound so sure."

He shrugged. Running his fingers up and down her throat, he let them slide against the wet silkiness of her skin in a sensualist's fantasy. "Considering the circumstances, I mean."

"Like where we are."

"Yes."

"And who we used to be."

"That, too."

"And two different life-styles."

"Unfortunately."

"So what do you think will happen?"

He bent his head. "Hell if I know."

"Poor Mac." She touched his hair, her voice pitying. "Always so stuck in the facts you can never see the dream."

"That's what the past day has been for me—a dream. But Christmas is over. The roads will probably be passable tomorrow. We've got to face reality."

"Of course. I never said differently."

Her apparent calm confused him, angered him. Did it all mean so little to her? "You're taking this with amazing sangfroid."

"And that surprises you?" Rising to her feet, water and suds streaming off her body, she smiled tenderly down at him as he knelt beside the tub. "That's because, Mahoney, I am in possession of certain facts of which you are apparently unaware."

"Such as?" he asked, standing. His fists were perched on hips in a belligerent attitude.

She placed a small wet hand in the center of his chest, then leaned toward him. "Our physical relationship is too wonderful and rare to give up lightly."

"*That* I know."

"Two capable people can accomplish anything they want, *if* they want it badly enough."

"I know that, too. At least in theory."

"All right, smart aleck, do you *know* that I'm in love with you?"

His voice was strangled. "Uh, I had considered the possibility."

"Liar." She leaned forward and dropped a light kiss over his heart. "You'd never look that close for fear of what you might find. But I do. Love you, that is. I always have." More kisses peppered his chest, teased at his nipples. "Madly. Passionately. Eternally."

Dread and exultation mingled in equal measure. "Marisa, I'm not sure what—"

Her lips stopped whatever he was going to say. "Shut up, Mahoney. No demands. Only let it grow, if it will, before you try to drown it with a shower of cold reality. Then we'll see."

Stunned, caught in an emotional tsunami, he found her nearness and her nudity and her honesty were more than he could resist. He stepped into the tub and wrapped her in his arms, luxuriating in the feel of her against his bare chest. Then he sank down, sweatpants and all while pulling her to a seat on his lap. He caught her face between his hands and found her lips.

"You're crazy, Mahoney!" She was laughing, gasping, her face flushed with the instantaneous arousal his touch always evoked. Shoving down his pants, she wiggled provocatively, inciting his body to riot as water lapped over the sides of the tub.

"You're the one who's in love with a madman, so does it matter?"

Sighing in pleasure, she took him into herself. "Not one whit."

"Is Mommy your girlfriend now?"

Marisa choked on her orange juice. "Nicky!"

"He was kissing you again. I saw him." Over his empty cereal bowl, the boy gave Mac a narrow look, man-to-man. "Well, is she?"

"Uh, I guess you might call her that." For an intrepid man of the world, a seasoned reporter who'd faced all kinds of situations with cold-blooded equanimity, Mac looked definitely rattled.

"My friend, Chad, says that's what mommies and daddies do." Oblivious to his mother's scarlet countenance, Nicky asked Mac, "Is that right?"

"Uh, yeah. Something like that."

"As much as you been kissin' Mommy?"

Mac couldn't stifle a grin. "More."

"Yuck." Nicky made a face, then shrugged. "I guess she likes it ... so are you going to be my daddy now?"

Marisa found her tongue. "Nicky, that's for grown-ups to talk about, not little boys. Now excuse yourself and go brush your teeth. Then you can turn on the cartoons for half an hour."

"Well, is he?"

"Nicholas!" The warning in her voice was clear.

"Oh, okay." The boy climbed down from his stool and stalked out of the kitchen while muttering under his breath about dumb grown-ups and unanswered questions. Marisa grabbed his breakfast bowl, emptied the leftover contents into the sink, then buried her face in her hands in chagrin.

"Sorry," she mumbled.

Pushing aside his own bowl, Mac came up behind her and clasped his arms around her waist. The front of his jeans brushed against her denim-clad bottom. His tone was wry. "I have to say that was the first time I've ever been given the third degree by a five-year-old. Pretty grueling."

"I'm so embarrassed!"

"It was rather chivalrous on Nicky's part, I'd say."

"It's not me he's worried about. You can kiss me until doomsday for all he cares—"

His lips brushed her nape. "I'll give it my best shot."

"—but he's just lobbying for a father." She gave a weak laugh. "And I said no pressure. Sorry."

His voice was quiet. "Marisa. I might not mind."

She turned in his arms, her eyes hopeful as she took in his solemn expression. "You—you mean that?"

"The idea's growing on me." He stroked her cheek with his forefinger. "Fringe benefits aren't so bad. With enough flexibility, we ought to be able to blend two careers into a compromise we can live with. But I'm not much of a bargain myself. You might want to think twice...."

"In case you haven't noticed, this *is* twice, Mahoney."

"So it is." He pulled her close and kissed her, then buried his lips in the curls beside her ear. "We'll get it right this time."

"I love you, Mac." Her voice quavered with unshed tears, and her arms tightened on his broad back.

Although he hadn't said the words back to her, she knew he cared deeply. No man could hold a woman with such tenderness and passion and be indifferent. That he wanted them to be together was a major step, and his growing affection for Nicky was clearly apparent. The words she longed to hear would come later, if she was patient. At the moment, her cup overflowed with joy.

She gave him another squeeze. "I knew if you saw, if you *felt* what Nicky means to me, you'd understand, and you'd have to help."

"Help?"

She swiped at the moisture clinging to her lashes and beamed up at him, almost giddy with relief and an impossible happiness. "To protect Nicky from this Dr. Morris thing. You can't keep after this story, not now, not at Nicky's expense."

He stiffened and set her a little away from him. "I can't make that kind of promise, Marisa."

"What?" Dismayed, uncomprehending, she stared. "How can you say that? How can you care for Nicky, for me—and still pursue the thing that will hurt us most?"

"It's my job. Personal feelings can't come into it."

She jerked out of his grasp. "I don't believe you're saying this! After everything—"

"Is that why?" Mac's face turned stone hard. "I wondered."

"I don't know what you mean."

"Don't play dumb with me, Marisa. It doesn't become you."

"What?" She shook her head. "Make sense!"

"Why you slept with me." He gave a bitter laugh. "You said you'd do anything to protect the kid. I should have realized you meant it. Except I wasn't quite prepared for the depths of maternal sacrifice you'd sink to."

Marisa felt the blood drain from her face. "That's vicious. And totally untrue. You know how I feel—"

"I know that you're a talented actress, and a desperate, if misguided, mother."

"Listen to yourself! You never gave that—" she snapped her fingers "—for my dramatic ability. Now I'm a femme fatale? Get a grip, Mahoney. My feelings were, and are, genuine. Even a fool can see that!"

"Oh, I realize there was a certain amount of pleasure involved—an unexpected perk, I guess—but don't insult me by telling me that the thought never crossed your mind that making love with me might insure my cooperation. I mean, I made it pretty clear from the start I was still attracted. Maybe you hoped you could convince me to kill the story altogether, pretend I never found you, or even help you to keep running when the roads clear."

She hesitated, but it seemed brutal honesty was what he wanted. "Maybe at first, for one wild moment, but no later, Mac, and never seriously. You know in your heart I wouldn't use you like that."

"Do I?"

She lifted her chin. "Even if I was desperate enough to have considered it, thinking it doesn't make it true."

"That's rather convenient reasoning, don't you think?"

She ground her teeth. "How can you be so infuriating! I thought we'd reached a certain level of trust here. Was I mistaken?"

"I can't say at the moment. But if we're going to be together in any fashion, you're going to have to trust me to do what's right about the Dr. Morris story."

A chill ran through her, and she hugged her arms. "You—you're asking a lot of me. Maybe too much."

"Then we didn't have as much going as we thought, did we?" Grim mouthed, he shrugged. "Christmas dreams—all cheap tinsel and fleeting splendor—have a way of fading in the ordinary light of day."

"No. I can't accept that it was only that." Pain made her voice tight. "Unless . . . unless you're afraid."

"Me? Of what?"

"Getting too close. Learning that your black-and-white world does have gray areas where Mahoney's Rule of Truth doesn't hold up."

He made a sound of disgust and went to the coatrack for his jacket. "Keep telling yourself that, honey. Maybe one day you'll believe it. I'm going down to get my Jeep."

"Oh, I see." Angry, she taunted him. "You get to ask the hard questions, but I don't? That's really fair. So who's running away now?"

"Give it a rest, Marisa. I'm just going after my vehicle." His eyes were dark with challenge. "The question is, will *ou* still be here when I get back?"

The door slammed behind him, and Marisa blinked, stunned by the rapid turnabout. How could he be so bull-headed? It was incomprehensible to her that he could be practically proposing in one breath, and then repudiating everything that had happened between them in the next.

She gripped the edge of the sink, breathing hard, staring out at the slowly melting snowscape. The man was a luna-tic, obviously. Demented. A fiend who lived to torture those who tried to get close to him. And none of that changed the fact that she loved him with all her heart.

But how to reach Mac on this issue? And how to con-vince him that his doubts and accusations about her feel-ings were baseless? If only she had someone to advise her.

Desperate, not really knowing who she was about to dial, she reached for the phone, only to find that there was still nothing but silence on the other end. She slammed down the receiver. No one, not her agent, her co-workers, not even Gwen or Uncle Paul, could give her any help now. She was in this on her own, and she had to find a solution.

Still agitated, Marisa stalked into the den, wringing her cold fingers. Nicky sprawled on the floor, small chin propped in his hands, watching a legion of heroic crime fighters saving the world from destruction. If only real life could be so simple!

The huge Christmas tree in the corner seemed rather shabby in the thin morning light. Its wilting foliage and tat-tered paper decorations mocked all the hopeful thoughts and holiday wishes they had put into its creation.

Marisa plucked a bandanna off one branch, then an-other. Yes, Christmas was over. The whole thing would have to go, and so would she and Nicky. Where they would end up was another question entirely, but before they left, Un-cle Paul's lodge had to be set to rights.

"Nicky," she said, "come help Mommy. We have a job to do."

"When's Mac coming back?"

"I don't know, honey. Soon."

Marisa and Nicky had spent a comfortable morning working together, taking down the stately tree, washing and drying linens, dusting and generally tidying the lodge. They'd tossed the leftover sugar cookies to the birds, but somehow Marisa couldn't bring herself to discard the rest of the decorations. She'd found a box and carefully packed away paper chains and tinfoil stars as if they were cherished heirlooms. Now, as Nicky folded the last of the clean dish towels, she inspected the cupboards and compiled a list of supplies that would have to be replaced.

"What I said..." Dressed in corduroys, his new chaps and his six-guns, Nicky carefully stacked his last towel on the pile on the kitchen counter. "You know, at breakfast? It didn't make him mad, did it? I mean, he wouldn't leave without saying goodbye?"

"No, of course not!" She pulled her head out of the pantry, she set down her pen and pad and placed a reassuring arm around her son's shoulders. "He's probably just having more trouble than he thought getting his Jeep out of the snowbank. He'll be back soon. And if he isn't, you and I will take a walk down the hill to see what's keeping him, okay?"

"Okay. Maybe when he gets back he'll help me build another snowman?"

Troubled, Marisa frowned. This was just the kind of attachment that she'd been afraid of. "Nicky, Mac wasn't angry about your questions, but we haven't known him long enough to make any kind of plans with him. Do you understand?"

"You like him, don't you, Mommy?"

"Oh, yes. Very much." She sighed. "But sometimes grown-ups have problems that aren't easy to work out. I'm glad you and Mac are friends, but you can't hope for more than that. Not yet, Nicky. If you do, you might end up disappointed and sad."

The boy laid his fair head on her shoulder and plucked at the cuff of her shirt. "Would you be sad, too, Mommy?"

She had to swallow hard. "Yes. Yes, I would. But people have jobs and obligations, and sometimes things like that can get in the way of feelings. We'll be leaving the lodge soon, Nicky. We'll just have to wait and see what happens."

"We're going home? I want to show Gwen my stuff!"

She hugged him. "I know you do. I miss her, too. But I haven't decided yet. We may take some extra vacation days. Just you and me. That would be fun, right? I have to think some more about it."

"Well, okay." He fastened bright blue eyes on her face. "But can I take my sled?"

"Absolutely." She nodded. "Even if we have to tie it to the car like a big old hood ornament!"

"I'd rather let it ride on the back seat," he said, a solemn half-pint judge. "I don't want to scratch it up!"

"Of course, you're right. We'll take very good care of it."

"Then that'd be okay." He pulled away. "I'm going to go draw some more pictures."

"Good idea. And thank you for helping me."

As Nicky disappeared into the front of the lodge, Marisa picked up her writing materials again. The mundane chores involved in closing up the lodge had done much to calm her internal upheaval following Mac's departure, but Nicky's innocent questions brought her nerves to strumming apprehension again.

She noted on her list a few more supplies to replace, then set the pad aside with a frustrated sigh. She put the kettle on the stove to boil water for a cup of tea and tried to think.

She was a reasonable person. Or could be, if she remained calm about the situation. Maybe she *was* expecting too much for Mac to completely give up his pursuit of the Dr. Morris exposé. After all, the man had backbone when it came to injustices. And his notion of what and who he was would not tolerate slacking off from the pursuit of anything he found important, no matter how dangerous, no matter what it cost others, no matter what it cost him personally. She knew that about Mac, and loved him for his drive and total commitment, didn't she? How could she expect him to change in so fundamental a fashion just for her and Nicky?

Well, she did. She wanted it to be easy. Marisa dipped her tea bag thoughtfully, acknowledging to herself that it just wasn't going to happen. All right, hard as it was, she could accept that. Now what?

What reasonable people did when they were at an impasse was reach a compromise, she told herself. After sugaring her tea, she slowly sipped the hot beverage, letting the sweetness slide down her throat, welcoming the caffeine kick—anything that would help her focus on the central issues.

So what were they? She loved Mac and wanted to be part of his life, and she had to protect Nicky. And Mac *had* offered to be her voice, to interview her so that her side of the story could be told, too. There were worse things than having a sympathetic listener on your side while the rest of the media wailed. She and Nicky were victims, too, and solid, supportive public opinion in her corner could be very important.

But could she afford such a gamble? She could still go to Monaco. Nicky would be safe from any legal technicalities there. She had plenty of wherewithal for an extended stay, even at the sacrifice of her career, but Mac was right about running away from problems—it was never a solution. It might have taken her ten years, but she'd finally learned that lesson.

Marisa dumped the remains of her tea down the drain and squared her shoulders. If she truly loved Mac, she had to trust his judgment and be confident that he'd see her and Nicky through this crisis to the best of his ability. As frightening as she found the prospect, she knew if Mac was standing at her side, loving her, she could make it through anything.

Now all that remained was convincing a very skittish man of that fact.

The sound of a vehicle grinding up the slope in four-wheel drive drew her to the window just moments later. A cherry red Jeep with Mac at the wheel swept into the driveway, cutting swaths through the sloppy snow. He rounded the lodge and pulled to a stop at the garage in back of the house.

Marisa stirred the canned chili she'd put on the stove to heat, checked that Nicky was still engrossed in his artwork, then reached for her own jacket. The sooner she told Mac about her decision, the better she'd feel. She prayed he'd be receptive.

Outside, the snow was melting. Moving toward Mac, Marisa's boots met soggy earth, and she felt confident that even with Gwen's regular tires, she'd be able to drive the little sedan down to the main highway with no trouble.

But maybe Mac would recommend their staying another day or two, just to talk things over and plan strategy. The idea of spending another night in his arms made her cheeks heat and her breath come shorter. She was actually puffing when she reached the Jeep, only to find it empty.

"Mac?" Puzzled, she looked around. The garage door was shut and showed no sign of recent entry, and the woods beyond the building were silent and motionless. She looked back toward the lodge, wondering if he'd walked around front while she was stirring chili. Then she heard him, his deep voice muffled and indistinct.

Had he taken up talking to himself, or was he still so coldly furious at her that he needed to curse in private? Timorous, but overwhelmed with both curiosity and the need to get this matter over with, she followed the sound around the corner of the garage. What she saw and heard stopped her dead in her tracks.

"I'm telling you, Tom—" Mac had propped his shoulders against the plank wall of the garage, his booted feet were casually crossed, and he was gesturing with one hand toward the trees. In the other, he held a small, high-tech cellular phone pressed to his ear. His conversation was heated. "I don't care what the network says! I told you before, I'm handling Marisa Rourke *my* way. They'll get what they want. But when I'm good and ready, understand? And not one minute before!"

Snippets of thoughts flashed through her shocked brain.

. . . *always doing some chores* . . .

. . . *Tom, I told you before* . . . *before* . . . *before* . . .

The realization hit her with the force of a runaway freight train. The lying, misbegotten newshound had been in contact with his slimy media cohorts all along!

She moved before she was fully conscious of her actions, and caught Mac unawares when she wrenched the wretched instrument from his hand and then heaved it with all her might into the underbrush.

"What the hell?" Mac rounded on her, the tinny voice from the telephone bleeping from the bushes.

She was so enraged, so hurt, so *betrayed*, she could barely breathe. Her fists clenched at her sides, she fought the urge to pummel him into a pulp.

"How could you?"

Color mounted his cheekbones, but his voice held steady. "It's not what you think."

"What I think is that you are the worst kind of hotshot, riding roughshod over anything and anyone who gets in the way of your *story*." Her voice was acid, scathing in her contempt and disgust. "You're a cowboy all right—a cheap-trick news jockey with the personal code of a rattlesnake!"

"That's enough, Marisa."

Her eyes glittered. "Well, here's a news flash for you, Mahoney—hang up your spurs, the ride's over!"

Nine

"Nothing's really changed, has it? The first sign of trouble, you turn tail and run."

Marisa looked up from the underwear she was folding into Nicky's suitcase to find Mac leaning against the doorframe of the boy's bedroom. His parka hung open, and a snowy residue dotted the knees of his jeans. He'd evidently had to dig awhile to locate the cellular phone that dangled from his left hand. "You're on very thin ice here, Mahoney," she said coldly. "I'd advise you to shut up."

Feeling as though her face had turned to marble, she folded a pair of Nicky's pajamas smartly, then added them to the suitcase. Nicky was gathering his toys downstairs while she packed their belongings. Fully aware that Mac tracked her every move from his position in the doorway, she held herself together by sheer force of will, refusing to shatter in front of him. When he spoke, his voice was low. "Are you going to let me explain?"

"The only thing I want before I close the lodge is for you to take out that damned Christmas tree." Steeling herself, she met his gaze. "And burn it."

"Marisa—"

"Since you're traveling light, it won't be any problem for you to be ready to leave in, say, one hour? This holiday hotel is closing for the season."

"Dammit! Will you give it a rest?" He stepped inside the bedroom and tossed the phone down in the middle of Nicky's bed in disgust. "You're jumping to conclusions."

"Just as you did about why I made love with you." She glowered at him, hot color flooding her pale cheeks in a wave of renewed rage. "According to your theory, it was because I'd do anything to save my son—even prostitute myself to the point of lying about being in love with you."

"Well, did you?" he demanded harshly.

"I never lied about that!" Eyes blazing, she vented her fury. "Not that you deserve an answer, since you've been sleeping with the star in a kind of reverse casting-couch routine so you can get the 'big scoop' and clinch your contract!"

"You've got it all twisted."

"Oh, right. Tell me getting that close to me wasn't an advantage. After all, what makes better copy than a fugitive celebrity? And now you've definitely got the inside track to all the juicy details! Are you going to tell your viewers I like wall-bangers and being kissed on the—"

"Marisa!" He shoved his hands through his hair. "Cut it out, please!"

"Stuff those lofty ideals, Mahoney. I'm sick of you and your holier-than-thou attitude. You've sacrificed everything you ever stood for or believed in for the god of the Almighty Ratings! Tell me, who sank the lowest here?"

"I swear to you, I haven't been feeding Tom information."

"Tom Powell, your producer? No wonder you were so reluctant to promise to help me! You've been in contact with him since you got here, right?"

"Only peripherally."

Incensed, she jammed the rest of Nicky's things into the suitcase without bothering to fold any more of them and slammed it shut. "What the hell is that supposed to mean?"

"That I've been holding him off with a lot of false leads and mumbo jumbo so I could retain some control of the story—"

"Oh, just like you did on 'Jackie Horton Live.'" Her voice was snide.

"Will you listen!" Mac exploded. He caught her by the upper arms and forced her to face him. "That happened against my better judgment. That's why I've been stalling Tom, so I could figure out something while I tried to make some damn sense out of what was happening between us!"

"How very gallant of you to lie to me in such a pleasing fashion." Her lower lip trembled. "And to think I'd decided to give you the interview you wanted, knowing I could count on you to be fair to me and Nicky. Obviously I'm the world's greatest fool!"

"You had? The interview?" He looked slightly stunned.

"Oh, yes," she said bitterly, jerking free of his grasp and taking a step backward. "If I loved you, I had to accept you the way you are—upright, moral, a pillar of integrity—and not expect you to sacrifice an important story simply because it might cause irreparable harm to me and my son! I decided you had to know the truth."

His eyes narrowed. "What truth?"

"Are you ready for this, Mahoney?" She lifted her chin in defiance. "You were right all along. Five years ago, Mr.

and Mrs. Victor Latimore paid Dr. Franco Morris quite an exorbitant sum to purchase a white male infant.''

"A black-market baby."

"Yes."

Mac's mouth was a grim line, his voice flat. "So all your claims of innocence have been lies."

She was instantly fierce. "After the way you've deceived me, don't you dare cast that stone, Mahoney! I'd lie to *God* to protect my child!"

"He's not really yours."

Marisa's hand flew to her heart, and she swayed as his blunt words stabbed her. "Yes, he is," she whispered. "I didn't know what Victor had done."

Mac shucked out of his parka and threw it on the bed, irritation and skepticism in every movement. "That kind of defense won't wash, Marisa."

"It's the truth!" She dashed the beginnings of tears from the corners of her eyes and glared at him. "Victor arranged the whole thing. I never even heard Dr. Morris's name until that afternoon on 'Jackie Horton Live'!"

"So how did you find out?"

"The night I left L.A., after that woman—Elsie something, from Louisiana—came forward claiming to be Nicky's birth mother, I went through Victor's things, stuff that had been packed away since the accident. He'd even hidden it from me, but I found it, taped to the underside of his desk—all the papers that he'd signed, the canceled check, everything." She groped for the edge of the twin bed and sank down.

"So you ran, and ended up here."

"What else could I do?" Misery and guilt clouded her expression. "I didn't know what Victor had done, but it was my fault."

"How do you mean?"

She looked up, her eyes wide and haunted. "I didn't love him enough. All that time, it was still you, Mac."

Breathing hard, he dropped to a crouch in front of her and took her hands in his. "Oh, honey..."

"I was lonely. And he was so kind to me." Her fingers tightened on his in growing urgency. "You have to understand. Victor was a good man, and I really cared about him. I thought it would work, but he always knew that there was a piece of me he could never touch, that belonged to someone else—to you—and it ate away at him."

"You couldn't hold yourself responsible for what he felt."

"I tried to understand his jealousy, his possessiveness." She shook her head, and her slow, hot tears dropped onto their joined hands. "I think Victor thought if we had a child together it would forge something between us that hadn't been there before. But nothing we tried worked, and finally we found out that it was Vic's problem, and it made him crazy. So we talked about adoption, but you know the usual channels have long waiting periods. I think he was so desperate, that's why he went to Dr. Morris."

"So he could give you the child he couldn't produce himself."

"Yes. We both wanted the baby, and it never occurred to me to question how quickly the adoption had been arranged. Victor had always had a way of doing things easily, so it didn't seem unusual."

"Enough money can make anything easy."

She looked into Mac's eyes. "Don't judge him too harshly. It was because he was afraid he'd lose me. But he never really had me, and when he finally understood that, he—" she drew a painful, shuddering breath "—he got in his car and drove it off the side of a mountain."

"Marisa, no." Mac found a place on the bed beside her and gathered her quaking form close.

"We'd had a fight..." Slumped against his shoulder, she wept silently.

Mac's voice was thick. "You've been carrying all this guilt around for three years? Look, Marisa, you can't do this to yourself. It was an accident, and that's all."

"If I'd been honest with him, if I hadn't run away from my true feelings, maybe he could have dealt with it better. Maybe he wouldn't have been driven to go outside the law, and maybe I wouldn't be losing Nicky right now."

"That's not a foregone conclusion."

Wiping her eyes, she drew away from Mac, then rose and went to stare out the window at the thawing, sun-splashed landscape. Her voice was husky with the effort it took to admit the truth. "What Victor did—what we did—was wrong. I can't defend it. Nicky is my heart, but he has never really belonged to me, just as I never belonged to Victor."

Behind her, Mac was silent for a long moment. "So the question I asked when I first arrived hasn't changed. What are you going to do?"

She turned slowly to face him. "Is that the reporter asking? Or the man who nearly proposed this morning?"

He looked startled, then his features hardened, and he admitted, "I'm not sure."

Her heart plummeted to her feet, and the old impulse to run, the almost irresistible urge to avoid pain, rose within her in its place. But in the past days and hours, she'd faced her innermost demons, the memories and feelings that had circumscribed her personality and forged her existence, and she'd been strong enough to come through that journey to self-knowledge, not exactly unscathed, but whole enough to endure, to persevere. She'd hoped earlier that she and Mac would face the difficult question of Nicky's future together. From his reluctance to admit his feelings for her, to even consider the repercussions of that failure in the equation that was their relationship, it appeared that would not be the case. She could accept it and move on, not because she wanted to, but because she had no choice.

"I can't stop you from leaving, Marisa," Mac was saying, "but taking Nicky away isn't going to solve anything. In fact, it could make things worse. There might even be criminal charges involved in fleeing across state lines and such."

"I understand that."

He frowned, misunderstanding her hard-won composure, amazed at the calmness in her voice. "But what? You're still going to risk it? Running away—"

"We're going home."

"What?"

"Back to L.A. To face the music." She raised her chin. "I'm hiring the best lawyers I can find, and I'm going to fight for my son, Mac. Even at the risk of losing him—" Her voice choked, but she swallowed and went on. "I can't condemn Nicky to a life on the run. I've learned that no matter how far you go, there are some things you just have to face head-on."

His expression relaxed, and a gleam of pride and admiration shone in his eyes. "That's good, princess. Real good."

"You need to learn the same lesson, Mac."

He lifted his eyebrows. "Me?"

"All those years covering the globe, never planting roots, always on the go, haven't you figured out you were running, too?"

"It was my job—"

"Come on, Mahoney, just for once, shine the light of that brutal honesty of yours into your own heart. After all the lies we've told each other, we at least deserve to be truthful about this. When will you stop running from the fact that you still love me?"

"I thought I'd shown you—you know how I feel about you."

"Do I?" She shook her head regretfully. "I know you desire me. But I don't think you trust me, and I know that's my fault. I can't guarantee I'll never hurt you again, Mac. That's not how life works. I *can* promise, though, that I'll do my darnedest never to let you down, and to let you into my most secret heart. Then, when you have to leave me to go do your job, I'll be strong enough to know you'll come back to me when you can."

"What about the absences, the loneliness? What if you get fed up, then take off again?"

"Maybe the girl I was at twenty would do that, but I've grown up. I don't want you to be anything but what you are, Mac, and if that means understanding your work is important to you, then I can do that, and I expect the same respect in return. But it's as if you're afraid I'll somehow suck the soul right out of you if you care too much."

"You know I want to be with you."

"But you're always holding something back, don't you see? It's what I did to Victor, and I saw what it cost him. I do love you, Mac, but half a loaf isn't enough for me anymore."

His jaw worked. After a minute, he stood. "I guess that's it then."

The tiny hope she'd clung to that somehow she could reach him flickered and died. Blindly she went to Nicky's suitcase and picked it up. She was proud that her words held only a faint tremor. "You'll know where I am, if you change your mind."

"This isn't where I meant it to go between us." His voice was ragged. "Look, I won't abandon you to the wolves in L.A."

"Still after that exclusive interview?"

He cursed. "Forget about that! But I'm the reporter who broke this story, and I've got influence. I can smooth things over—"

"No, Mac." She touched his arm. "This is something I have to face alone."

"Marisa, if only..." For a timeless moment, Mac stared at her, his eyes clouded with despair. Then something inside him snapped, and he snatched her into his arms and lowered his head to kiss her with a desperation matched only by her own.

When he released her, she touched her lips, dazed, blinking at the tears prickling behind her eyes. "Oh, Mac..."

He moved away from her. "I'll take out that tree."

"Mommy, Mommy!" Nicky barreled into the room, his eyes round. He braked to a stop, instantly sensing the palpable tension between the two adults. "What's the matter?"

"Nothing, honey." Marisa stroked her son's fair head and essayed a strained smile. "I—I was just telling Mac goodbye."

Disappointment made the boy's lower lip pucker. "He isn't coming with us?"

"Not this time, partner," Mac said, his tone gruff.

"Then when?" the boy demanded.

Desperate to end this train of conversation, Marisa interrupted. "Nicky, was there something you wanted?"

"Oh, yeah, I forgot. The pot on the stove's smoking!"

Marisa clapped a hand over her mouth and groaned, "Oh, blast, the chili! Maybe it's not too scorched to eat."

Features stiff, Mac cut her off at the door, his eyes bleak with regret. "Forget it, princess. Some things just can't be salvaged."

Ten

I've never loved anyone but you.
  Don't give me that!
  Walk away if you dare—then we'll both have nothing.
  The passionate words of two estranged lovers faded, and the auditorium monitors went dark on the final nominee. A handsome leading man in a designer tuxedo leaned into the podium microphone. "And the *Daytime Digest* award for Best Actress goes to…" Paper crackled. "Marisa Rourke!"

The glitzy, glamorous crowd exploded into enthusiastic applause, and "Time Won't Tell"'s lush theme song swelled from the orchestra.

In her seat, Marisa gasped in astonishment and buried her face in her hands. When she found her feet, her face was wreathed in well-practiced smiles. Beside her, Paul Willis, tanned from his Indian sojourn and looking very debonair at seventy, bussed her on her cheek in congratulation and encouragement, then gave her a push toward the stage.

"Give 'em hell, honey," he said, grinning, his silver hair gleaming in the barrage of spotlights following the star.

Heart beating like a drum, Marisa made her way down the aisle, carefully negotiating steps—especially treacherous for someone dressed in a strapless, crystal-studded white sheath—praying that she wouldn't disgrace herself and inwardly cursing her agent, Carlene, for insisting she attend tonight's gala televised Hollywood awards ceremony.

It was a month into the new year, but since her arrival home, there hadn't been a day that she hadn't been hounded by the paparazzi, especially after Nicky's alleged birth mother had filed a custody suit against her. What followed was a flurry of countersuits, DNA testing that proved Elsie Powers was indeed Nicky's birth mother, and a media field day over Victor's dealings with the nefarious Dr. Morris. All Marisa had really wanted to do was lie low and pray while she and the lawyers and the social workers and the courts fought it out over Nicky's future, but Carlene had been adamant.

"You'll thank me for it later, Marisa. Despite anything you can do, you're in the spotlight now, and if *you* don't control things, *they* will...."

The presenter, Kane Morgan, a celebrated prime-time actor turned director, was a friend. He met her on the last step and escorted her to the podium as the crowd rose to its feet. Pressing the gleaming statuette into her hands, he kissed her lightly on each cheek and murmured in her ear, "Keep your chin up, champ."

"Thanks, Kane." Clutching the heavy gold trophy, she smiled her gratitude, sensing that his support was more than just acknowledgment of her award. After all, no one in this community was unaware of her circumstances. As she stepped to the podium, the crowd noise increased even more, and she had to swallow on a wave of emotion. These were her peers, and whether they were celebrating her professional accomplishments or merely pouring out sympathy for one of their own, she was touched.

"Thank you." She cleared her throat, waiting for the audience to settle into their seats again. "Thank you so much. I'd like to thank *Daytime Digest* and the many fans of 'Time Won't Tell' for making this honor possible. Playing Dinah Dillman has been one of the joys of my life, and I'm both proud and humbled that she has touched so many others. Of course, there are many to thank, beginning with Eric . . ."

While rattling off the names of her fellow actors and crew, Marisa gazed out into the audience and absorbed the moment. Capturing this award was a long-awaited dream come true, a symbol that she had arrived, and yet the triumph was empty. What price success if she lost her son as she had lost the man she loved?

Marisa had not seen or spoken to Mac Mahoney since the day they'd driven down from the Sierras. She told herself it was best this way—a clean break, no messy scenes—but she'd been surprised. Mystifyingly, he'd kept the story of her runaway attempt to himself. She supposed he'd decided that after everything that happened between them, the decent thing for him to do was pursue his Dr. Morris exposé from some other angle rather than face her again. She ought to feel grateful, but it still hurt like hell, and she missed Mac more than she could ever have imagined.

As badly as she longed to run and hide from the pain, however, that was impossible. The hearing to determine whether the adoption Victor and Dr. Morris had arranged should be overturned and who should be awarded custody of Nicky was only days away now. Her son needed her, whatever happened, and she couldn't afford to let her broken heart interfere with that.

"...so once again, I want to thank you all," she finished. On the point of turning away from the podium, she swung back to the mike and blew a huge kiss. "And that's for my son, Nicky, who's watching at home. You can go to bed now, sweetheart. Mommy's got her prize!" The audience laughed appreciatively while Marisa smiled and gave a final wave. "Thanks again."

The music came up on cue. Gratefully Marisa accepted Kane's arm and allowed him to lead her offstage for the mandatory appearance in the press room. "Ready to face these jackals?" he muttered, squeezing her hand, his dark face etched with concern.

She shrugged bare shoulders. "As ready as I'll ever be."

"Marisa, if there's anything I can do, anything at all..."

"Whenever you want to film a happy ending for me, I'll be glad to oblige." Her quip was a trifle wobbly, but drew an answering smile from the director.

"Don't we both wish it was that easy."

"It helps to have friends like you." She pressed his hand in return. "Thanks, Kane. I'll let you know."

He assisted her to a low dais from which the winners were expected to address the members of the press congregated in the room, then gave her an encouraging wink. "You do that."

The gaggle of entertainment reporters and camera people crowded around, firing questions and rolling video for the late news. "Miss Rourke, how do you feel?"

"Wonderful. Honored." She clutched her trophy closer to her breast. "And amazed. I truly didn't expect—"

"Miss Rourke, there was some talk of a prime-time comedy series offer. Are you going to stay with 'Time Won't Tell'?"

She shook her head. "I'm flattered to be mentioned in the same breath as these projects, but really, I'm very happy where I am, and I have no other plans—"

"Miss Rourke," boomed a tabloid reporter in the rear of the group, "what about this Elsie Powers claiming to be your son's birth mother? Did you know she's in negotiation with Jackie Horton for an exclusive interview?"

Another reporter piped in, "How is the boy dealing with the controversy? What have you told him?"

"Do you expect a prolonged court battle? How high will you take any appeal? To the Supreme Court?"

A pushy blonde in tortoiseshell glasses elbowed her way to the front. "What about the Adopt-a-Child Foundation? Is it true that you're being replaced as spokesperson?"

Overwhelmed, Marisa reached deep inside herself and found a measure of composure in the place that had been strengthened and tested by her fight to win Mac's love. She had learned that even in defeat and loss, one could find the fortitude and the grit to endure. And she had cause to give thanks for her acting ability. "I'm sorry, everyone, but as you know, this particular subject is in litigation, so it's not appropriate for me to comment."

Cordial and cool and in control, and certainly not running any longer, she smiled and firmly changed the subject. "Now, did you know that next month's story line is a CIA infiltration plot that reunites Dinah with her first love? Folks, this ain't your mother's soap opera anymore...."

Mac Mahoney punched the remote. The television on the faux walnut motel bureau went black and the overblown music of yet another self-serving awards show was silenced. Stupid, inane posturing, a photo op for the terminally vain—that's all they were. He hadn't meant to watch the show at all, had no reason to. No, he'd merely been channel surfing and, by the sheerest coincidence, had found the familiar face of an old flame.

"Yeah, right, Mahoney." Muttering at his self-delusions, Mac dropped the control on the rumpled bedspread, irritably punched up his pillows and tried to catch a little shuteye. The flight to Madrid for his new assignment left in a little over six hours. This close to Dulles International, however, the roar of jet engines never abated, so closing his eyes was really an exercise in futility.

And torture.

Because behind his lids all he could see was Marisa as she'd appeared on the TV screen, looking sexy and glamorous in a long white column of a dress, her bare shoulders gleaming like ivory, her hair swept up in some sort of casual, tousled twist that made a man's fingers itch to take it down again. A vision that pointedly reminded him that she'd become as remote and untouchable as the moon for a working stiff like him.

Mac scowled, his mind replaying the scene over and over. Her gracious little speech. The way her glittery gown clung to every familiar curve. Her accepting that damned award from a pretty-boy actor, then letting the guy kiss her, fondle her—on national television, for Pete's sake!

He kicked the sheet off his nude body and rolled over. Snow lay outside the window, but he felt overheated and feverish. Cursing, Mac switched on the lamp, reached for the pack of cigarettes on the nightstand and lit one. The smoke tasted acrid and bitter on his tongue. It suited his mood.

Not a damn thing had gone according to plan since he'd left California, since he'd let Marisa walk out of his life again. Mac flopped onto his back and stared up at the ceiling. Who was he trying to kid? Hell, he'd driven her away with his craven insensitivity, just as he had ten years ago.

And he couldn't have been more brutal about it if he'd taken a baseball bat to her skull.

Oh, afterward, when it was much too late, he'd tried to make it up to her in his own small way. Tom Powell had gone ballistic when he realized Mac was serious about killing Marisa Rourke's sensational runaway story.

"Just a Christmas vacation? Are you nuts?" Apparently on the brink of a fatal cardiac infarction, Tom had tugged at his thinning hair in a frustrated rage. "You're blowing the chance of a lifetime! Don't expect me to pull your fat out of the fire with INN if you don't come through for them."

"Fine with me." With a shrug, Mac had walked out.

He'd severed his increasingly codependent association with his longtime producer, been kicked off the Dr. Franco Morris black-market-baby story and had the INN contract he'd counted on rejected, all within a twenty-four-hour period. What concerned him was that he didn't really care.

No, it was the image of Nicky in the rear window of the car as he and his mother drove away that haunted Mac. A little cowpoke's upside-down smile, the final wave of a chubby hand and the realization that the pursuit of ideals to the exclusion of relationships and emotion and love could leave a man as empty and dry as a locust's abandoned shell.

The tip of the forgotten cigarette scorched Mac's knuckles. Growling, he stubbed it out and reached for his clothes. Sleep was beyond him. He slid into his slacks, then grabbed the jumble of keys and change off the dresser. His fingers hesitated on a tinfoil star. After a month in his pants and jacket pockets, it was bent and battered, the lettering, Sheriff Mac, nearly invisible, but he couldn't bring himself to toss away his final link to Marisa and her son.

Mac critically examined the bare-chested man he stared at in the dresser mirror. He hadn't had any real trouble landing a short free-lance assignment in Spain, but the thought of it filled him with ennui. There wasn't much left of the enthusiastic, idealistic reporter he'd once been. When had he lost his perspective? When had barreling ahead with a story, heedless of the human cost and just to prove to the world that Mac Mahoney could *produce,* become more important than the story itself? When had causes begun to outweigh the people involved?

No wonder Marisa had bailed out. Who could blame her? Mac shook his head. No, that wasn't fair. He was the one who'd been so damned afraid of what she was making him feel that he'd run for cover like a spooked jackrabbit.

Was that where he'd gone wrong? Maybe the sheer impact of all that he'd seen and done—the human misery, the suffering—had somehow activated a defense mechanism that short-circuited his ability to empathize, simply to enable him to survive the experience. The catch was, by turning off his emotions, he'd squandered the ability to see the most important part of every story—the human part—and his full-steam-ahead, damn-the-torpedoes stance had made him into an instrument of destruction, the disrupter of innocent lives, not the savior he thought himself. Even more tragically, he'd lost the courage to give himself totally to someone who cared for him, and that failure had cost him the woman he loved.

Again. And this time, there was little hope that she'd ever forgive him.

Staring at his reflection, Mac knew that it was past time to reevaluate his priorities if he ever hoped to redeem himself. As badly as it hurt now, his time with Marisa had done him an invaluable service by forcing him to take a long, hard look at himself.

He didn't particularly like what he saw.

Marisa was out there battling a mess he'd at least partially created, trying, as any mother would, to do the best for her child, and he'd left her alone to do it. Well, he could change that much, at least. There were still things he knew how to do, answers he knew how to find and an ending that he had to write.

For Marisa's sake. For Nicky's. And ultimately, for his own.

Mac reached for the telephone and dialed. "Reservations? There's been a change of plans."

The private conference room was a ten-by-ten foot cubicle that smelled of new floor polish and old sweat. Outside in the halls of the Los Angeles County Courthouse, bustling footsteps and loud voices went about the business of justice. Inside the room, Marisa sat quietly, wiping her damp palms on her sedate wool suit and listening to her petite, dark-haired agent, Carlene Mendez, argue with the Latimore Corporation attorney.

"Well, I think this is highway robbery!" Carlene said heatedly, thumping her fist on the grimy tabletop. Her scarlet nails matched her lipstick and power suit. "Isn't there a name for this kind of thing, Mr. Windham? Extortion, maybe?"

"Miss Mendez, please." Michael Windham wiped his middle-aged forehead with a precisely folded handkerchief, then flicked the locks on his briefcase and passed Marisa a sheaf of papers. "Ms. Powers's offer. They are willing to accept these terms before the hearing convenes this morning."

Numbly Marisa took the document and scanned the paragraphs of legalese with no comprehension. She waved a hand over it. "And it says...?"

"Basically what we've already discussed. The child, Nicholas Victor Latimore a.k.a. Elwin Andrew Powers, will be held in joint custody between the two of you. There will be specified visitations, summer holidays and the like, and a settling-in period for Nicholas to get to know Ms. Powers. And, of course, there is the monetary settlement from you, child support in lieu of damages.''

Carlene snorted, her fiery Latino temperament getting the best of her. ''Damages! Why isn't this Powers woman suing Dr. Morris? He's the one who duped her into giving up her baby. He's the one who should be paying, not Marisa!''

Windham took off his bifocals and polished them with the handkerchief. ''As you are aware, Dr. Morris has filed for bankruptcy, taken a plea bargain and is currently serving a mandatory ten to twenty years in the state's minimum security facility at San Pedro.''

''Well, I still don't see—''

''Carlene.'' Marisa touched her friend's arm, and the other woman subsided instantly. ''It's not the money. From all accounts, Ms. Powers is a decent person, but she doesn't have much materially. I have the money to give, especially if it allows Ms. Powers to provide for Nicky in a comfortable manner.''

''Sorry,'' Carlene murmured, then sank into the chair beside Marisa. ''It's just so unfair!''

''In my experience, life is rarely fair,'' Windham said. ''We do well if we make it even fractionally equitable.''

Marisa swallowed. ''And your recommendation, Michael?''

''Considering the recent custody decision in Michigan, I feel that taking the case into open court might very well be a mistake,'' he said cautiously.

''I might lose Nicky altogether.''

''It's a distinct possibility, considering the, er, questionable circumstances of the adoption itself. As painful as it is for you to hear this, and even though you are basically an innocent party, in these instances the courts tend to favor the birth parent's rights. The adoption can be overturned."

"I—I see."

"But that doesn't mean it has to be that way, does it?" Carlene protested. "Look, Windham, if you're afraid to battle this thing out before a judge, we can find someone who isn't!"

He bristled. "My dear Miss Mendez, I assure you—"

"Tell Ms. Powers I agree."

Both Windham and Carlene stared at Marisa.

"Are you certain?" the lawyer asked.

"Marisa, you can't! Nicky—"

"Nicky is my primary concern." Although Marisa's voice was quiet, inside she was screaming. But succumbing to emotion wouldn't accomplish anything. "As abhorrent as I find the idea of turning my baby over to the care of another woman—even a mother who loves him as much as I do—I can't risk losing Nicky completely. It's not ideal—in fact, I hate everything about it—but since I can't run away from reality, I have to try to do what's right and deal with it in the only way I can. Nicky is young and flexible. He'll adjust. We both will, because we have to."

Carlene looked aghast. "You can't mean to give up without a fight!"

"It's a workable solution, and I will do my best to make it work so that Nicky is subjected to as little trauma as possible. He's very confused and frightened right now as it is. If he was forced to go live full-time with a total stranger..." Marisa bit her lip and fought back the tears gathering behind her eyes. "I won't put him through that. This way, I'll be there to help him at least part of the time."

Windham retrieved the documents and closed his briefcase. "In that case, I suggest we go inform the judge."

Feeling numb, Marisa forced her features to stillness and followed the attorney down the corridor and through a phalanx of television reporters and film crews poking microphones and camera lenses in her direction. It was excruciating. Even at this moment, faced with surrendering her son, she would not be allowed to grieve in private.

She entered the sanctuary and relative quiet of the courtroom where the hearing was to be held with a feeling of vast relief. It was quickly replaced by shock as she caught sight of a familiar whiskey-dark head near the front of the spectators' benches.

Mac. The joy that spouted like a geyser caught Marisa unawares and released her from the numbness. Handsome in jeans and sport coat, he was achingly familiar, and she drank in the sight of him, then practically floated down the center aisle behind Windham. She barely noticed Carlene taking a place in the first row of seats. The only thing that was important was that Mac had come to her. When she needed him most, he'd come. To share the burden, to bear her up, to love—

On the brink of calling out his name, Marisa saw him turn in his seat to speak to the chestnut-haired woman next to him. Dressed in a plain black skirt and jacket, her thick hair clipped severely at her nape, she listened to Mac with solemn attention.

Realization struck Marisa, and she caught a sharp, painful breath as hope died. It was the story, of course. Mac Mahoney's reputation was at stake, and the latest installation of the Dr. Morris melodrama was to be played out before Judge Margaret Lassiter in just minutes. Where else would he be at such a crucial moment? It seemed fitting that he had somehow dodged the edict barring reporters. After all, nothing had ever stood in the way of his stories.

Coupled with the knowledge of what was to follow, this was almost more than Marisa could bear. Steeling herself, she kept her features emotionless as she passed Mac, not even bobbing when he noticed her and half rose. At her frozen stare, he subsided again, his expression unreadable.

Marisa took her seat next to Windham at the defendant's table, burying her shaking hands in her lap and staring resolutely at the empty judge's bench as if nothing more important existed in the world than counting the rows of walnut molding decorating the stand. She was only vaguely aware when Elsie Powers arrived, accompanied by her attorney and another man, who appeared, from the proprietorial grasp he kept on Elsie's arm, to be a very close friend, indeed.

Marisa stirred herself to covertly inspect Nicky's birth mother. She was a pleasant-faced blonde in her early twenties. Her companion looked like a California surfer type, sun-bleached hair hanging long over the obviously uncomfortable collar of his dress shirt and tie.

These were the people who would become a part of Nicky's life, and hers. Briefly closing her eyes for strength, Marisa prayed that she could bear it with grace. She refrained from looking back at Mac for support only with the most supreme effort.

Windham had risen to speak quietly with the other attorney. They conferred briefly with Elsie and her friend. Their nods and patent looks of relief conveyed acceptance of the terms. At that moment, the bailiff stepped forward to intone his "Oyez, Oyez."

Judge Margaret Lassiter swept into the chamber with a flap of black robes and took her seat, and the bailiff read the case name and number.

Michael Windham spoke first. "Your Honor, may it please the court, Counsel would like to approach the bench."

The judge, an imperial figure with salt-and-pepper hair, gestured, and both attorneys came forward to perform a quiet duet explaining the agreement reached and the plaintiff's intention of dropping the suit.

It's happening, Marisa thought. Staring at her knotted hands, she knew that nothing in her life would ever be the same after today.

Then there was another voice, female with a Southern inflection, rising over the lawyers' murmuring. "Your Honor, I beg indulgence as an officer of the court. May I approach?"

Marisa swiveled in her chair to find the voice belonged to Mac's chestnut-haired companion. The woman calmly made her way toward the bench. Mac's lean features held an attitude of expectancy, but the rest of the onlookers— spectators, attorneys, even Elsie and her friend—all wore puzzled frowns.

Judge Lassiter looked down her regal nose at the interloper. "Your name and business?"

"Lieutenant Gillian Kennedy, Lafayette, Louisiana Police Department, ma'am. I have a warrant for the arrest and extradition of Elsie Suzette Powers on felony charges of jumping bail and sale of minor children."

The courtroom erupted in a flurry of speculation. Marisa could hear Carlene's high-pitched voice behind her, the angry cry from Elsie, the vociferous protests of her lawyer. Confused, stunned, Marisa met Mac's gaze, and he nodded. Although to interpret what he meant was beyond her capabilities amid the tumult, a tremor of awareness and longing vibrated deep in her chest.

The judge banged her gavel, demanding order. "Lieutenant Kennedy," she said, "this is highly irregular. Tell me what bearing on the case—"

"Your Honor, Ms. Powers is a fugitive under indictment in her home state." The policewoman's voice was melodious, but firm and carrying. "I have in my possession sworn depositions of witnesses who testify that she has sold not one, but two infants, the one for which she is charged in Louisiana, and the child in question in this case."

Pandemonium rocked the room. Elsie screamed an obscenity and her companion added his curses. Judge Lassiter slammed her gavel furiously against the desk, then gestured to her bailiff. Her voice was grim over the noise. "All parties, in my chambers. *Now.*"

"It's all over."

Stunned, Marisa let Michael Windham shake her hand. "I can't believe it."

Beaming, the lawyer blotted his forehead and escorted Marisa from the judge's chambers into the anteroom, where a secretary worked at her typewriter and a small contingent of interested parties awaited them. "You heard what Judge Lassiter said," Windham replied. "Suit dismissed. Powers is under arrest, the D.A. is very interested in pressing charges in California, and from what that policewoman said, Elsie faces a sure conviction back in Louisiana. That, of course, entails her permanently forfeiting all her parental rights to Nicholas. There's no doubt the social welfare folks will find his staying with you is in the best interest of the minor child."

"And I can file for a proper adoption."

"Right. We'll get on it immediately, but I don't foresee any problems whatsoever." Windham patted her shoulder. "Congratulations, Marisa."

"It's true then?" Carlene materialized in front of them and enveloped Marisa in a hug. "Tell me everything!"

Over Carlene's shoulder, Marisa caught a glimpse of the man lounging near the doorway. His eyes, hazel green and brilliant, pierced her, held her. Disentangling herself, she absently pushed Carlene toward Windham. "Ask Michael."

Marisa left her agent shooting questions at the well pleased lawyer. Light-headed, the surroundings and the events of the morning feeling surreal, she crossed the room as if she were walking under water, her gaze never leaving Mac's.

He shoved his hands into his jeans pockets and gave her a crooked half smile. "All's well that ends well, eh, princess?"

"You did it." Her voice held a note of wonder.

"Who, me?" Shrugging, he kept his hands where they were, as if he might be tempted to reach for her otherwise and refused to take the chance. "No, I didn't do any—"

"Michael told us what Lieutenant Kennedy said, Mac. How you backtracked into Elsie Powers's past, and found out who she really was and her boyfriend, too. How she'd sold Nicky to Dr. Morris in the first place, and that after Jackie Horton's show, when they realized the soap opera star the doctor had mentioned was *me,* how they planned to use Nicky again to wring the Latimore fortunes dry."

"Hey, I just dug around. It's my job, you know."

"Yes, I know." *Tell me it's more than that,* she begged silently. *Tell me!*

Mac shifted his feet and cleared his throat. "You'll be able to get on with things now."

"Thanks to you." Unable to stop herself, she touched his arm, and her fingers trembled. "I don't know how I can ever repay you."

He went very still, and his voice was gruff over the tick-tick-tick of the typewriter. "You don't owe me anything. It was the least I could do after...well, hell, there were no guarantees about what I'd find, you know, but it was my responsibility to find out the *whole* truth."

"And you did, and brought it to the authorities. I still can't believe it."

He gave her a cocky grin that somehow looked rather strained, and shrugged again. "You know I'd do anything for a story, and you can't pay money for this kind of drama."

The story. Oh, yes, the big scoop. Foolishly she'd almost forgotten. Her hand dropped away. "I—I see. Well, thank you, anyway."

"Mac." Gillian Kennedy, fresh from the judge's chambers, approached with her hand outstretched. "Gotta run. Appreciate your help."

"No problem, Gillian." They shook hands. "Have a safe trip home."

The policewoman turned to Marisa. "Ms. Rourke, I'm glad everything worked out for you. Mac here sang yours and Nicky's praises the whole time we were digging up the dirt on Suzette—Elsie, I mean."

"Thank you for everything, Officer."

Gillian gave Marisa a considering look, woman to woman, then tilted her head in an almost imperceptible nod and smiled warmly. "You've got quite a champion in your corner. Good luck. See ya'll around." With a wave she was gone.

"That's one real savvy lady," Mac commented. "Damn good cop."

"She cares about people."

"Yeah."

"Like you."

Mac looked startled for a moment, and a muscle in the side of his jaw worked. "I guess so. Maybe I'd forgotten that for a while, but I'm going to do my damnedest to remember it from now on."

The conviction in his tone filled her with pride, and she smiled. "I don't doubt it."

He pulled back his cuff to check his watch. "I've got to go."

A weight settled on Marisa's chest and constricted her breathing. Her whisper was filled with dismay. "Where?"

"Madrid. I'm already a few days late for an assignment."

She swallowed. "Oh. With INN?"

"No, I had to let that one pass."

"Because you never filed another report on me." She knew by his expression her guess had hit the mark. "Well, thank you again. And good luck."

Whatever he saw in her eyes made him groan softly, then cup her cheek with his hand. He pressed a soft kiss to the corner of her mouth. "Bye, princess. Tell Nicky I said howdy."

With one last caress of his thumb, he turned away. Frozen, Marisa watched him disappear through the office door and down the courthouse corridor. She saw that Carlene and Windham were still in a deep discussion and noticed that the secretary had paused in her typing to give her a curious glance, but she could only stand there paralyzed with despair. *He's leaving! How can he do this to me, to us? Running away from a chance at happiness! Running . . .*

Something snapped, and Marisa was off, slamming through the door. Ignoring the cluster of reporters and photographers lingering outside the judge's chambers, she sprinted after Mac, her high heels clicking on the tile. She caught up with him at the elevators, swung him around and shouted up into his astonished face, "Tell him yourself, you coward!"

"Marisa." Her name was a warning. His eyes darted with alarm to the descending horde of avid reporters. "Not now."

"If not now, when?" she demanded, punching him in the chest with her forefinger. "If not here, where?"

He scowled at the whirring cameras, the bouquet of microphones thrust at their faces, the questions hurled at their heads like a barrage of mortar shells.

"Ms. Rourke, have you got a statement?"

"Hey, Mac, what's the deal?"

"Is it true Elsie Powers is going to jail?"

"Were they trying to extort money from you, Ms. Rourke?"

"How much were you willing to pay for your child?"

"What's your relationship with Mahoney?"

Mac caught Marisa's arm and pulled her around to shield her from the onslaught, at the same time punching the elevator button in desperation. "Come on, *come on.*"

Marisa couldn't contain a wild laugh. "What's the matter? Can't take the heat, Mac? It's about time you had a taste of your own medicine! Ladies and gentlemen of the press, Mac Mahoney has a statement he'd like to make—"

"Princess, for God's sake, not now!"

"Yes, *now.*" She was frightened and furious and determined, terrified that she'd never have another chance. Words she knew by heart tumbled from her lips. "Don't you dare try to walk away from me, Mahoney. If you do, then we'll both have noth—"

The elevator doors slid open and Mac pushed her inside, then hit the Close Door button to keep anyone from following them. "What are you saying?" he growled. "Something out of a script, isn't it?"

"Yes, you damn fool!" She was almost crying. With a leap forward, she pulled the Emergency Stop toggle, then staggered as the car lurched to a halt between floors. Steadying herself with a hand on the wall, she glared at him. "The reason it's so real is that I helped write it!"

"Huh? You did what?"

"You heard me. It comes from the heart, cowboy." A tear spilled over and trickled down her cheek. "I've never loved anyone but you. And I never will."

"Marisa." He closed his eyes as if in pain.

"You saved my son for me. For that alone I'd give you my life, but it's always been so much more." She went to him and looped her arms around his neck. "Look at me, Mahoney."

He did, and she saw his Adam's apple bob as he swallowed.

"Nicky needs you. I need you. Your terms, Mac. Any way you say. Just—just don't shut me out of your life, please."

He placed his hands on her shoulders and his forehead touched hers. "Marisa, I'm tired of fighting this."

"Then rest in me, and let me be your homecoming. Fly as far away as you have to. I promise I'll be here when you get back."

Her face framed with his hands, he looked down at her with eyes that glittered with high emotion. "Just a glutton for punishment, hmm?"

"We paid ten years for the mistakes we made. I think we've both learned our lesson."

"You're reckless, lady, and foolhardy. My track record proves I'm something of a slow learner."

She gave him a tremulous smile. "You're worth it."

Mac looked thunderstruck, and Marisa saw his inner struggle in his expression, then the moment of revelation and surrender. The words sprang rough and unvarnished from his soul. "My God, I love you."

Hands in his hair, she pulled him close, her reply almost soundless. "I know."

His kiss was hungry, masterful in its triumph, humble in its profound relief. They clung to each other, sealing the bonds, broken once and now rewoven into something even stronger. Lost in the mystery, it was a long time before either one of them became aware of the insistent buzzing of the emergency phone.

Mac lifted his head slightly, but didn't release her. "I think we're being paged."

"Ignore them. It's the only way to deal with obnoxious media types." Her lips nibbled at his, and she strained against him.

"Like I said—reckless, foolhardy, and now add shameless to that list."

"You want shameless?" Laughing, pouting, she hooked one leg around his calf and gave him a provocative look. "How about this—will you marry me, Mahoney?"

"Does Nicky come with the offer?"

"Uh-huh."

"Lady, you got yourself a deal. I only hope you know what you're getting yourself into."

"Oh, I think I might have an inkling," she purred, her happiness overflowing.

He looked worried. "What if I can't—"

"We'll make it work, Mac. It's a pact. No running, no hiding, just us learning every day how to love each other."

His arms tightened around her. "That, I can do."

"Good." She picked up the buzzing telephone but let it dangle unanswered, then punched the highest numbered button.

Amused, Mac arched a dark eyebrow at her. "Are we going somewhere?"

"You guessed it, Mahoney." With a glorious smile, she settled into his arms again. "Get ready for the ride of your life."

Epilogue

Juggling an armload of wrapped presents, Mac quietly let himself into the beach house just as Christmas Day dawned over Malibu.

"Daddy!"

A fair-haired six-year-old tornado launched himself down the stairs before the door clicked shut. Mac dumped his packages just in time to scoop the boy up and toss him, shrieking with laughter, toward the ceiling.

"Howdy, partner! Merry Christmas! How 'bout a kiss?"

Nicky squeezed Mac's neck and bussed his stubbly cheek. "Santa's been here!"

Mac felt a twinge of regret. "That's great. What'd he bring?"

"Dunno yet."

"We waited for you."

Mac glanced up to find his wife watching from halfway

down the staircase. Dressed in a frilly eyelet peignoir, with her blond hair tumbled around her shoulders, Marisa looked sweet and virginal, an appearance at such odds with the passionate reality of their physical relationship that Mac felt his blood heat just looking at her.

"You didn't have to do that," he protested.

As Nicky wiggled from Mac's arms, she came down the stairs and lifted her face for her own kiss. "Don't be ridiculous. We knew you'd make it. How was Mexico?"

"Hot. Dirty. Courageous. Humbling."

"Your report on the earthquake was fantastic. If that family you interviewed doesn't get people to open their hearts and their pocketbooks to aid the survivors, well... well, there's no such thing as Christmas spirit!"

Tired as he felt, Mac grinned and slipped out of his jacket. He tapped his fist lightly on her chin. "Thanks, slugger. But you're prejudiced."

"Guilty as charged."

Nicky had Mac's hand and was tugging him toward the glass-walled living area that faced the Pacific. A Christmas tree decorated with paper chains and cowboy bandannas reigned in a position of honor. Mac and Marisa had found the house soon after their wedding and loved it, preferring to start their married life unencumbered by old memories.

"Come on, Daddy," Nicky said. "Let's go see what Santa brought!"

Within minutes, Mac was comfortably settled on the overstuffed sofa, a cup of coffee in one hand and his other arm around Marisa's shoulders. Nicky's cries of delight over a shiny red two-wheeler, assorted cartoon action figures and a brand-new Stetson hat filled the air, along with the flash of Marisa's camera and the pleasantly muted sounds of Christmas carols.

There wasn't a day in the last eleven months that Mac hadn't counted his blessings. Thank God the hardheaded woman he loved had possessed the courage to fight to make them a couple again. He shuddered to think what his life would be like without her and Nicky, without his family. It made the hard things he chose to face in his work bearable; it made the separations tough, but the reunions all the sweeter.

Mac smiled to himself. Not that there would be as many separations in the future. No, it looked as though his work on the Dr. Franco Morris story, as well as the reports he'd filed this past summer from the Ukraine and South Africa were going to net him the correspondent's position at INN, after all. The contract they'd offered was hefty, but it was having more control of his working schedule he truly appreciated. Marisa's own studio hours were demanding enough, and might even become more so, especially if she decided to seriously consider the latest offer of a prime-time series. Being able to be around more of the time was Mac's Christmas gift to Marisa and their son.

"Tired, Mahoney?" Marisa's head rested on his shoulder. "You're awfully quiet."

"Just thinking what a difference a year makes."

She placed a hand on his thigh. "Regrets?"

"Are you kidding? Not a one. If nothing else, that picture is worth the whole experience."

"You're not going to ever let me take that down, are you?"

"No way, José." Mac grinned, letting his gaze roam to the framed front page of a national tabloid mounted in a place of honor among an assortment of Marisa's acting and his own journalistic awards. The picture splashed across the front page showed the two of them wrapped around each other in the open doors of an elevator. In Mac's book it was a classic.

"Mommy?" Nicky bounced on the sofa beside them, his eyes bright. "Are we still going to have pizza for Christmas dinner?"

"Absolutely. What else are traditions for?"

"And we're gonna go up to the lodge with Uncle Paul and make snow angels and go sledding, huh, Daddy?"

Mac nodded. "New Year's weekend. That's a promise, partner."

Nicky's expression was satisfied. "Swell. Mommy, can I give Daddy his present now?"

"That might be a good idea," Marisa said, casually picking at the lace on her sleeve. Smiling to himself, Mac wondered what she'd been cooking up.

"Okay!" Nicky pulled a bulky package from behind the Christmas tree. "Open it, Daddy!"

"Think I should?" Mac winked. "Maybe I ought to wait."

"No, now!"

Teasing the boy with a constant stream of nonsense, Mac gingerly tore off the huge red bow and peeled off the colorful wrapping paper. When he pulled open the flaps of the cardboard box, he froze. "Oh, my God."

"Isn't it a beaut?" Nicky demanded, hopping up and down in excitement. "Mommy and I picked it out together! Go on. Take it out of the box."

Mac lifted the most beautiful Tonka dragline he'd ever seen out of the package and set it on the floor. His throat felt thick. How had she known?

"Better late than never, huh, Mac?" Marisa asked softly. "Like us."

"I don't know what to say."

"That's an unfortunate affliction for a reporter," she teased gently. "How about 'I love you.'"

"You already know that."

"Yes." She smiled. "I do."

"There's something else," Nicky interrupted. "Look in the bucket, Daddy!"

"Sure, sport." Mac cleared the gruffness from his throat and ruffled the boy's hair. "Let's see what we've got here." Mac turned the small crank that opened the dragline's bucket, and two small fuzzy somethings fell to the carpet. Puzzled, he picked them up and, for the second time in as many minutes, found himself utterly speechless. It seemed absurd that a grown man could be made to feel so helpless by the sight of a pair of tiny knitted booties. "A—a baby?" he croaked.

"These things do tend to happen, Mahoney. Especially when you—" Finding Nicky's bright blue gaze on her, she broke off with a blush. "Well, never mind that now."

"It's going to be a baby brother or sister," Nicky explained importantly. "Aren't you glad? Me and Mommy are."

"Yes, son, I am very glad," Mac replied, feeling as though his heart would burst. "And if your mommy will come here, I'll show her just how much!" Nicky muttered something about mushy stuff and went back to inspect his Christmas toys as Mac pulled his unresisting wife onto his lap. "You're my very own Christmas miracle, you know that?" he whispered. "I love you, Marisa."

Her eyes bright, she touched his cheek tenderly. "Merry Christmas, Mac."

Nicky looked up from his bike to see his mother being thoroughly kissed by his new father. Somehow, when they did it like that, it didn't seem so bad. In fact, it gave him a

warm feeling right in his middle that he didn't mind at al
Sometimes the very best presents didn't come in boxes.

Looking up at the tall Christmas tree, Nicky gave a se
cret smile. "Thank you, Santa."

* * * * *

Get Ready to be Swept Away by
Silhouette's Spring Collection

Abduction
&
Seduction

These passion-filled stories explore both the dangerous
desires of men and the seductive powers of women.
Written by three of our most celebrated authors, they are
sure to capture your hearts.

Diana Palmer
Brings us a spin-off of her Long, Tall Texans series

Joan Johnston
Crafts a beguiling Western romance

Rebecca Brandewyne
New York Times bestselling author
makes a smashing contemporary debut

Available in March at your favorite retail outlet.

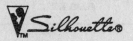

Take 4 bestselling love stories FREE

Plus get a FREE surprise gift!

Special Limited-time Offer

Mail to Silhouette Reader Service™

3010 Walden Avenue
P.O. Box 1867
Buffalo, N.Y. 14269-1867

YES! Please send me 4 free Silhouette Desire® novels and my free surprise gift. Then send me 6 brand-new novels every month, which I will receive months before they appear in bookstores. Bill me at the low price of $2.44 each plus 25¢ delivery and applicable sales tax, if any.* That's the complete price and—compared to the cover prices of $2.99 each—quite a bargain! I understand that accepting the books and gift places me under no obligation ever to buy any books. I can always return a shipment and cancel at any time. Even if I never buy another book from Silhouette, the 4 free books and the surprise gift are mine to keep forever.

225 BPA AARS

Name	(PLEASE PRINT)
Address	Apt. No.
City	State	Zip

This offer is limited to one order per household and not valid to present Silhouette Desire® subscribers. *Terms and prices are subject to change without notice.
Sales tax applicable in N.Y.

UDES-94R

MONTANA
Mavericks

Stories that capture living and loving
beneath the Big Sky, where legends live
on...and mystery lingers.

This January, the intrigue continues with

OUTLAW LOVERS
by Pat Warren

He was a wanted man. She was the beckoning angel
who offered him a hideout. Now their budding
passion has put them both in danger. And he'd do
anything to protect her.

Don't miss a minute of the loving as the passion
continues with:

WAY OF THE WOLF
by Rebecca Daniels (February)

THE LAW IS NO LADY
by Helen R. Myers (March)

FATHER FOUND
by Laurie Paige (April)
and many more!

Only from **Silhouette®** where passion lives.

Is the future what it's cracked up to be?

This January, get outta town with Marissa in

GETTING A LIFE: MARISSA
by Kathryn Jensen

Marissa was speeding down the fast lane, heading nowhere fast. Her life was a series of hot parties, hot dates…and getting herself out of hot water. Until, one day, she realized that she had nowhere to go but… home. Returning to her hick town wasn't exactly her idea of a good time, but it was better than dodging phone calls from collection agencies and creepy guys. So Marissa packed up her bags, got on the bus—and discovered that her troubles had just begun!

The ups and downs of life as you know it continue with

GETTING OUT: EMILY
by ArLynn Presser (February)

GETTING AWAY WITH IT: JOJO
by Liz Ireland (March)

Get smart. Get into "The Loop"!

SILHOUETTE®

Desire®

MAN of the MONTH 1995

Don't let the winter months get you down because the heat is about to get turned way up...with the sexiest hunks of 1995!

January: *A NUISANCE*
by Lass Small

February: *COWBOYS DON'T CRY*
by Anne McAllister

March: *THAT BURKE MAN*
the 75th Man of the Month
by Diana Palmer

April: *MR. EASY*
by Cait London

May: *MYSTERIOUS MOUNTAIN MAN*
by Annette Broadrick

June: *SINGLE DAD*
by Jennifer Greene

**MAN OF THE MONTH...
ONLY FROM
SIILHOUETTE DESIRE**

MOM95JJ-R

Robert...Luke...Noah
Three proud, strong brothers who live—and
love—by

THE CODE OF THE WEST

Meet the Tanner man, starting with
Silhouette Desire's *Man of the Month* for
February, Robert Tanner, in Anne McAllister's

COWBOYS DON'T CRY

Robert Tanner never let any woman get close
to him—especially not Maggie MacLeod. But
the tempting new owner of his ranch was
determined to get past the well-built defenses
around his heart....

And be sure to watch for brothers Luke and Noah,
in their own stories, COWBOYS DON'T QUIT
and COWBOYS DON'T STAY, throughout 1995!

Only from